Stick in the Mud

MEETS

Spontaneity

Stick in the Mud
MEETS
Spontaneity

RACHAEL
ANDERSON

USA TODAY BESTSELLING AUTHOR

HEA PUBLISHING

This is a work of fiction. The characters, names, incidents, places, and dialogue are products of the author's imagination, and are not to be construed as real. The opinions and views expressed herein belong solely to the author and do not necessarily represent the opinions or views of HEA Publishing, LLC. Permission for the use of sources, graphics, and photos is also solely the responsibility of the author.

ISBN: 978-1-941363-13-3

Published by HEA Publishing

For all the fans of the Meet Your Match series.
Bless you for your enthusiasm and support.

Other Books by Rachael Anderson

Novels

Prejudice Meets Pride (Meet Your Match, book 1)
Rough Around the Edges Meets Refined (Meet Your Match,
book 2)
Working it Out
The Reluctant Bachelorette

Novellas

Righting a Wrong (A *Ripple Effect Romance*)
Twist of Fate (A Holiday Romance)
The Meltdown Match

One

THE WHIRR OF the helicopter blades pounded like a subwoofer in Colton McCoy's ears, echoing off the surrounding, low-lying hills. Colton leapt over the gate and into position. Under the brim of his Stetson, his eyes scanned the horizon. It was only March, but the Nevada sun had been frying them all morning. With no clouds to temper the heat, the dry and barren desert outside of Silver Springs felt like a hot summer's day in Colorado. Nearly forty thousand wild mustangs chose to call this place home, and Colton had no idea why. The water was scarce, the shade nonexistent, and the sun unforgiving.

Across the narrow valley floor, his friend, Will, manned the other half of the gate. Will had to yell to be heard above the sound of the oncoming chopper. "You ready for this?"

Colton's muscles tensed and adrenalin pulsed through his body as he tugged the brim of his hat down and squinted into the early afternoon sky. Over the slight rise ahead, the whirring blades appeared first, followed by the round yellow and black body of the Robinson R22 chopper.

About two dozen mustangs crested the rise and charged toward Colton, stirring up dust into billowing clouds. The chopper followed close behind, coming dangerously close to the ground as the pilot guided the mob toward the enclosure. Fences lined each side of the small valley, creating a long, wide path that would usher the horses into entrapment.

Colton watched in awe, mesmerized by the untamed power and majesty of the approaching horses. As they neared the mouth of the enclosure, a beautiful chocolate mustang stopped and reared, slowing the other horses down. The mob began to change directions, away from the fencing, but the chopper quickly swung to the side, blocking the exit. At the same time, two trained horses were released not far from the mustangs. They darted through the fencing and toward the corral. After a moment of what seemed like indecision, the mustangs followed.

In a flurry of dust and pounding hoofs, they thundered past Colton. Wind from the chopper and horses whipped around him. He tugged the blue bandana tied around his neck over his mouth as a shield against the dust. Then he drove his shoulder into the gate, shoving it closed as quickly as he could. Will met him with the other half of the gate, and in a few deft movements, the two men had the horses secured in the enclosure. They stepped back just before a tan mustang crashed into the gate, fighting for its freedom.

The ground shuddered beneath Colton's feet as more horses attempted escape, but the fencing was strong and resisted their efforts. The pilot in the hovering chopper gave a quick wave before veering off to search for additional herds.

A month ago, when Will had asked Colton if he wanted in on a wild mustang roundup, Colton's response had been an emphatic yes. Get paid for rounding up wild horses? It sounded like an awesome, once-in-a-lifetime adventure to him. But now, as the horses continued to protest their captivity, the adventure lost its appeal.

Every year, the Bureau of Land Management removed thousands of wild horses from public lands. Too many horses drained the resources, making it necessary to control the population and keep the habitat healthy for the animals that remained. At the time Colton first learned about the program, it had made sense. But now, seeing the fear and belligerence in the eyes of the horses, he wasn't so sure. The words "unjust" and "wrong" came to mind.

Will clapped him on the back and grinned. "You don't see this every day. Pretty amazing, huh?"

"They are amazing." Colton watched as the animals began to calm down and accept their confinement. "I can't believe the BLM is going to stick them into a holding facility somewhere."

"Not all of them. A large chunk of them will be auctioned off for adoption."

Colton focused on the black stallion that seemed to be the leader of the group. He pranced around the holding yard in an antsy way, as though still searching for a way out.

Sorry, buddy. There isn't one. Better get used to those fences.

"You're looking a little sick," said Will.

"I'm feeling a little sick."

"If it helps, back in the day they used to poison horses to keep the numbers in balance. At least this way is more humane."

Colton grimaced. "That's supposed to make me feel better?"

"You could always adopt some of them. Give them a good home and all that."

"Maybe I will."

His friend chuckled and shook his head. "You and your tender heart. I can only imagine what your daddy would say if you showed up with a bunch of wild mustangs."

"I don't have to imagine. I know," said Colton, already hearing his father's voice in his head. *What in tarnation were you thinking? This isn't a charity we're operating, boy. It's a business. And those horses are nothin' but bad business.*

"C'mon," said Will. "The chopper will be back soon. Let's get these horses harnessed and loaded before they track down another herd."

As they started toward the opposite end of the enclosure, Will nudged him with his elbow. "You sure you don't want a turn in the heli? It's more exciting than closing gates, breathing in dust, and loading horses."

"Positive," said Colton. The farthest his feet had ever been from solid ground was on the high dive at the local community center. He'd been eleven at the time, and every step he'd climbed made his knees more wobbly, his breath more sporadic, and his heart race faster. By the time he'd reached the top, a full-on panic attack seized him. A friend had to help him crawl back down, and Colton had felt like a complete wuss in front of his entire fifth-grade class. He could get bucked off the back of a horse over and over again without breaking a sweat, but when it came to anything involving heights, he was brought to his knees every time.

Going for a thrill ride in the chopper was definitely out of the question.

"Out of curiosity," said Colton, nodding toward the enclosure, "how much do they sell for at an auction?"

"It depends. The wild ones usually go for a couple of hundred while the trained ones have sold for upwards of 10K."

"Ten grand?" Colton whistled.

"You're telling me," said Will. "Every year the Mustang Heritage Foundation holds a makeover challenge. One hundred wild horses go to one hundred trainers who then have one hundred days to train them. A contest is held right before the auction and all the horses are judged. Those that make it to the top ten usually go for thousands." He paused and studied his friend. "You should do it."

"Yeah right." But the seed had been planted, and Colton let it grow a little.

They arrived at the back of the enclosure, and Colton hopped over the two fences that created a chute leading from the corral to the truck. One by one, the horses would be ushered into the chute, harnessed, and loaded into the large cattle truck. It would be a rocky ride for the driver.

"You ever been tempted to compete?" Colton said as he checked over his side of the chute to make sure everything was secure.

"Me? Heck no," said Will. "I don't have the temperament for it."

Which was true. Will was about as patient as a thirsty newborn colt wanting his first taste of his mother's milk. Colton, on the other hand, enjoyed working with horses. He saw them as strangers wanting to be understood and known. Once he figured them out, there wasn't much a horse wouldn't do for him in return. In his experience, animals were easy to be patient with. People, not so much.

Colton finished checking the fencing and glanced up to see his friend watching him with a gleam in his eyes. "You're considering doing that challenge, aren't you?"

"Thinking's not the same thing as doing."

Will chuckled and moved to the back of the chute, getting ready to release the first horse. "It is if you're Colton McCoy."

Two

SUNSHINE II, SAMANTHA Kinsey's semi-reliable yellow Volkswagen Beetle, puttered to a stop in the driveway of her childhood home. A colorful crystal sun catcher in the shape of a firefly dangled beneath her rearview mirror—a goodbye gift from her talented, jewelry-making roommate.

"It'll bring you luck," she'd said. "Not that you're going to need it. You're the luckiest person I know."

Sam smiled as the crystals caught the light of the setting sun and refracted the rays into sparkling patterns across her dashboard. She *was* lucky. She had the world's coolest parents, wonderful friends, a fresh-off-the-press college degree, and a to-die-for job offer from *the* Jason Brecken Design firm in Manhattan. Her world felt like sunshine and bubbles and happy dances.

Leaving her car squished to the brim with everything from clothes, laundry baskets, fluffy pillows, books, picture frames, and her very large portfolio, she jogged up the walkway and burst inside, more than ready for her summer of fun to begin.

"Surprise! Your brilliant, amazing, and talented daughter is officially home," she called out. "Who's excited?"

A drab, hugless silence greeted her, along with the faint scent of vanilla from an elusive plug-in.

Sam's smile wilted. Where was everyone? Where were the yummy smells of Chicken Milano that her mother made every time she came home? Where were the hugs, the laughter, Kajsa and Adi's excited chants of "Sam's home! Sam's home! Hooray!"

Some welcome home this was. Had her mom gotten the days mixed up? Impossible. Becky Kinsey never forgot anything—especially when it came to her only daughter. The barren feeling in the house gave empty nesting a whole new meaning.

Sam dropped her purse on the counter and pulled open the fridge, making a face at the moldy cheese and rotten tomatoes that sat on the shelf in front of her. What was going on? Had her parents taken a vacation without telling her? No, they'd never do that . . . Would they?

She hunted through her purse for her phone and slumped down on a barstool, tapping out a quick text to her mom.

Where are you?

Her fingers drummed against the counter as she waited for a response. Who forgot their only child was moving home from college? Granted, they'd officially celebrated her graduation four weeks ago, on the actual day she'd walked across the stage, but Sam hadn't followed everyone home then. She'd stayed to work for three more weeks at the admissions office, then stayed an additional week to train her replacement. But now she was officially home for the summer. Surely this warranted another celebration. At the very least a welcome-home hug and some ice cream.

Sam stared at her phone, willing it to chime and vibrate

with an answer. After a few minutes of waiting, she tried calling. A few rings later, a recording of her mother's voice sounded in her ear, so Sam ended the call and tried her father. It went straight to voicemail. She shoved her phone back in her purse and shook her head. They'd probably gone out for dinner and a movie or something.

Wow.

Out the back window, the trees had become dark shadows against the graying skies. Sam sighed. She should probably unload her car and get settled before it got too dark. If her parents didn't call back soon, she'd order a pizza and invite Kajsa and Adi over to share it with her. At least they had a good reason for not being here to welcome her home. They now lived ten minutes away and were protected by the naivety of youth. Her parents, on the other hand, had no excuse. Neither did Kevin, Emma, Noah, or Cassie. They were all in big trouble.

Returning to the front porch, Sam's gaze wandered across the street. The lights were on at the Grantham's and a breath of smoke hovered above the roofline. When Sam drew in a deep breath, the faint scent of a barbeque teased her stomach. Kevin was grilling something that smelled way better than pizza. Hopefully, they'd made extra.

Leaving her things in her car, Sam jogged across the street and walked through the gate on the side of the house that led to the backyard. She sniffed the air and smiled. Barbeque chicken—one of her favorites. A flurry of voices sounded, followed by the slam of the back door. Sam rounded the corner to find a smoking grill and an empty patio. She knocked on the door before poking her head inside.

"Emma? Kevin?"

Lights came on, and everyone shouted in attempted-unison. "Welcome home!"

Kevin and Emma juggled their almost one-year-old twins, Noah's arm was slung around Cassie's shoulders, and

Adi and Kajsa shoved a balloon bouquet in Sam's hands before throwing their arms around her waist. Over their heads, Sam's father grinned and her mother shook her head with an expression of annoyed tolerance.

Sam's smile returned. Now *this* was a proper welcome home.

"You were supposed to come in through the front door," her mother said, gesturing behind her. "We had a sign and more balloons and everything ready to go. I should have known you'd follow your nose instead."

Sam didn't feel the least bit repentant. "I should have known you wouldn't forget to throw me a welcome home party. You had me going for a few minutes."

"Did you like the rotten tomatoes and moldy cheese?" said her mother. "I thought they were a nice touch."

"They were. You had me thinking you'd gone on vacation without me."

Everyone laughed and her father's arms came around her. "That's what you get for accepting a job in Manhattan. What kind of daughter moves across the country from her parents? It isn't right, I tell you."

"No, it isn't." Her mother moved to hug her next. "You're lucky we planned a welcome home party at all. You don't deserve it."

"Oh, c'mon," Sam said. "Think of all the fun we'll have when you come to visit. Broadway shows, Times Square, the Empire State Building, hot dogs—"

"Maybe I *won't* come," said her mom.

"*I* will," called out Emma.

"Me too," added other voices.

Her mom glanced around the room. "You're all a bunch of traitors. Just wait until your kids grow up and decide to spread their wings. It isn't nearly as exciting for the parents."

Noah gave Becky a sympathetic pat on the back before drawing Sam into a warm embrace. "You're going to take

New York by storm, but we're going to miss you around here."

"I'll miss everyone too," Sam murmured into his shoulder. "But my job doesn't start until the fall, and we have the entire summer to hang out before then. This summer is going to rock."

As she hugged everyone else and kissed the little twins on their cheeks, some of Sam's good mood faltered. After this summer, how long would it be before she saw these little ones again? How much older would they look? Would their eyes grow large with fear when she held her arms out to them? Would she lose her place at the top of Adi and Kajsa's Favorite People list? Would her parents grow accustomed to her absence and not miss her? Would the Granthams and Mackies become distant friends instead of family?

Sam craved the opportunities that would come with this job. She looked forward to walking the streets of New York, taking in the sights, sounds, smells, meeting new people, having interesting experiences, and learning what life was like outside of Colorado. But would it come at the cost of everything good and wonderful in her life now?

"Why the glum look?" Emma asked as she passed Maxwell off to Sam. The sweet, not-so-little guy was almost a year old, with large, gray eyes, thick eyelashes, and the pudgiest fingers and thighs ever seen on a baby. His hair was coming in lighter than his parents, and his cherub cheeks were as kissable as cheeks got.

Sam juggled him on her hip, amazed at how much more he weighed since the last time she'd held him. The kid was solid. "When I come back, he's going to be walking all over the place, isn't he?"

"Let's hope he starts before you leave," said Emma. "Crawling keeps them too close to the ground, and they find stuff my vacuum doesn't, which goes straight in their mouths. I'm really hoping that being upright cures that problem."

"You're just building your little immune system, aren't you, buddy?" Sam tickled Maxwell's tummy, making him break into a grin. His chubby arms swished up and down, and his fingers snatched at Sam's long, curly blonde hair, tugging it.

"Ouch." She laughed as she untangled her hair from his fingers. "You little stinker." She poked his belly again, and he giggled, making Sam fall in love with him all over again.

"You'd better not forget me," she said quietly.

Emma put an arm around Sam and hugged her close. "The only thing he's going to do is miss you, just like the rest of us. No one could ever forget you. You'll be home for the holidays and we'll call, text, and Skype all the time. So you go to New York and have the time of your life. We can't wait to hear all about it." She gave Sam's arm a squeeze before breezing into the kitchen to finish laying out the food.

Sam looked around, catching Adi and Kajsa snitching from a bag of Doritos. She joined them, snagging a chip for herself, but couldn't quite get it to her mouth before Maxwell's fingers closed around it, crushing it into little pieces.

"You really are a stinker," chided Sam as she captured his hand and cleaned it with a napkin before he could get it to his mouth.

Adi and Kajsa giggled.

"He tries to eat everything," said Kajsa. "Dad calls him a human garbage disposal."

As though trying to prove the nickname, Maxwell snagged her hair again and shoved his fist into his mouth. The girls giggled harder.

Sam swung Maxwell to her other hip, away from the food, and pulled her hair around to the side, trying to keep it out of his reach. "What's on the agenda for tomorrow, girls? Sidewalk chalk bonanza? Our annual swimsuit fashion show through the sprinklers? A mud pie contest, which we'll definitely need to keep away from Maxwell? Or we can always take the raft to the lake and work on our balance. What do you say?"

"The raft at the lake," said Kajsa quickly.

Adi's expression fell. "I have to pack."

"Pack?" Sam tugged her hair away from Maxwell again. "For what?"

"Cassie and me are going to an Irish dance competition in Chicago."

This was news to Sam. Bad news. "When?"

"Our plane leaves really early Sunday morning."

"For how long?"

"Two weeks."

"Two weeks!"

Adi nodded. "The competition is only for one of the weeks, but then we're going to do some fun things before we come back, like go to a really cool museum and a water park and eat lots and lots of pizza." Her eyes took on an excited sparkle the more she talked.

"That doesn't sound nearly as fun as hanging out with me," said Sam. "I'm going to miss you. Are you going too, Kajsa?"

"I can't." Her shoulder-length brown hair shook with her head. "I have to work."

"She would *rather* work," Adi added. "We invited her to come, but she didn't want to."

Sam frowned. "Are you even old enough for a job? You're only ten."

"Almost eleven. I help clean the stables at the McCoy ranch to pay for my riding lessons."

"Since when?"

"Since I turned ten and a half. Dad said I was old enough to earn my keep." She grinned. "Or at least my lessons."

"Sheesh," said Sam. "You have it rough. I didn't have to start working for art lessons until you two moved in." She glanced at Adi. "Let me guess. Cassie has you mop the dance floor and scrub the walls to pay for your lessons, right?"

"Sometimes." She giggled. "But mostly I just help her with gear days."

The girls were sounding way too responsible for the beginning of summer. Sam was almost afraid to ask. "Gear days?"

Cassie grabbed a chip before stealing Maxwell from Sam. She'd been smart enough to pull her strawberry blonde hair back into a bun, so Maxwell latched onto the collar of her shirt instead. "It's a store I hold twice a year for people to sell their too-small shoes and dresses to people who can't afford to buy new. Adi's the best helper ever."

Sam nodded. "Sounds like a good idea."

"The parents appreciate it," Cassie said, tickling Maxwell's tummy. "And speaking of jobs, Noah and I have a favor to ask you."

"Shoot." Sam popped a carrot in her mouth, appreciating that she could do it without adorable, pudgy little fingers getting in the way.

"As Adi probably told you already, we're headed out of town for two weeks, and Noah is in the middle of a big project at work. I'm hoping you won't mind hanging out with Kajsa while we're gone and making sure she gets to her job and riding lessons."

This wasn't exactly how Sam pictured her first two weeks of summer. She wanted to spend time with the girls, not wave goodbye to Adi and be Kajsa's chauffeur. But what else could she do? They were growing up whether she liked it or not.

"I would like nothing better than to taxi you around, Kajsa," Sam said. "But only if you promise to make some time for me after lessons and work."

"I'm usually only there for about four hours a day," Kajsa said.

Four hours! How far away was this ranch anyway? Was Sam supposed to hang out at the ranch and wait?

Cassie must have read her thoughts because she placed her hand on Sam's arm. "Don't worry. The ranch is only about a thirty minute drive from here. All you have to do is drop Kajsa off and pick her up when she's done. My aunt Jane is really good to call or text when Kasja's close to finishing up."

That sounds doable, Sam thought. "All right. Consider me your personal chauffeur for the next two weeks. I think I'm going to need to buy one of those cool-looking caps to make it legit."

Cassie laughed. "Thanks, Sam. I owe you big-time for this."

"Let the girls come with me to the lake tomorrow, and we'll call it even."

"Deal," said Cassie. "I'll gladly get all the cleaning and packing done so the girls can spend the day with you before we leave."

"Oh, and Noah has to help me unload my car as well," Sam teased.

"We'll all help," promised Cassie. "Just as soon as we've finished eating."

With that settled, Sam glanced around the room, hunting for Georgia. When she spied Maxwell's smaller twin sister in her mother's arms, she moved to steal her away. With any luck, Georgia would have better manners than her brother.

Three

A CLOUD OF dust followed Sunshine II as Sam navigated the winding dirt road to the McCoy ranch. The property was a hardy mixture of earth, shrubs, pines, grasses, aspens, and the occasional maple or oak. A lovely little stream babbled not too far from the road, and clusters of pink and white columbine bloomed here and there. Through a grouping of trees up ahead sat a happily situated rambler adjacent to a large barn and some other outbuildings. With clusters of horses grazing in the surrounding pastures, everything about the scene felt like Sam had taken a step back in time. It was hard to believe they were so close to The Springs instead of in the middle of Nowhere, USA.

"I can see why you like coming here," Sam said as they neared the house. "It's beautiful."

"Wait until you meet Maverick," gushed Kajsa. "He's the most amazing horse in the world."

Sam cast a sideways glance at her former little charge who wasn't so little anymore, though she still looked adorable in the brown felt cowboy hat she wore with matching brown boots. "Is Maverick the horse you usually ride?"

"No. I ride Whisper." She frowned. "He whinnies a lot."

"And his name is Whisper?" Sam had to laugh at that.

"Colton says he's proof that reverse psychology doesn't work on horses. What does that mean, anyway?"

"That the horse has a mind of its own." Sam nudged Kajsa with her elbow. "You two probably get along great, don't you?"

Kajsa nodded. "I like Whisper, but he's not Maverick. Someday I want to ride a horse the way Colton rides Maverick."

"You will. Just give it time. From what I hear you're a natural-born horsewoman." They pulled up to the house, and Sam stopped the car, looking around. "Is there a place I should park? Where do we go from here?"

"You don't have to come inside. I know where to go and what to do."

"Oh, okay. Well, have a fun day."

"I will." A gleam lit Kajsa's eyes as she slammed the door and jogged toward the house, leaving Sam alone in the car and feeling like she'd been rudely awakened from a happy dream in which she was the center of Adi and Kajsa's world. Last summer, Sam had taken an internship with a company called Vinyasa in South Carolina, so she'd only spent the sum total of a week with the girls. But those seven days had been crammed full of fun and adventures—from treasure hunts to a pie eating contest to building the world's most awesome sprinkler out of PVC pipe.

When Sam had first learned that Jason Brecken Design wouldn't need her to start until the fall, she'd anticipated an entire summer of those same fun-filled days. But now Adi had dance and Kajsa had the ranch, leaving Sam in the back seat of their lives—or, in this instance, the driver's seat.

Kajsa disappeared inside the house, and a loneliness took her place on the passenger side. Sam relaxed against the headrest and drummed her fingers on the lime, fuzzy steering wheel cover she'd gotten as a goodbye gift from a roommate. Soft, bright, and happy, it sent a very loud message: *Find something to do that will make YOU happy.*

Yes, that's exactly what she needed. This temporary "back seat" was Sam's last summer of freedom, her final hurrah before she had to settle down and become a responsible adult. She wasn't going to sit around like a pathetic lapdog, watching and waiting, hoping for some attention from the girls. With or without Adi and Kajsa, Sam was going to turn this summer into one that she could always look back on with bright, lime-green, happy memories.

In order to do that, she needed a list.

Sam rummaged through her glove compartment until she found a notepad and pen. In big, bolded letters, she spelled out "Summer Bucket List" then tapped the top of the pen against her lower lip as she looked around for inspiration. Her gaze landed on a horse grazing in a nearby pasture and a smile lifted the corners of her lips. She began writing.

> *Learn to ride a horse* (Maybe Kajsa could help her with that?)
> *Ride a bull in a rodeo* (You didn't have to be a professional to do that, right?)
> *Learn to country dance*
> *Have a summer fling with a cowboy*

Sam glanced around again but didn't see a cowboy anywhere on the premises. Okay, so maybe the ranch was providing too much inspiration. She quickly crossed out "with a cowboy." A summer fling with any cute guy would work.

The pen tapped against her lip again as she pushed her thoughts beyond the borders of the ranch—toward food, ice, airplanes, and purple dye. Her positive summer outlook had just been restored when a beefed-up engine rumbled up the drive behind her. Loud banging accompanied the sound, and Sam glanced in her rearview mirror to see a large, red Chevy hauling a beat-up white horse trailer that shook with every bang. Whatever animal was inside that trailer didn't like being confined. Was it a bull?

Another loud bang sounded, and the trailer shook again, making the Chevy shake as well.

Huh. Perhaps riding a bull wasn't such a great idea.

Sam was about to scratch it off her list when a good-looking man wearing a brown cowboy hat jumped from the cab of the truck. He took a few steps back and rested his hands on his hips, surveying the volatile trailer. Well-defined arms and shoulders stretched the fabric of his t-shirt, drawing her attention. He looked to be about her age. Maybe a little older. Since he didn't appear too anxious to free the animal, Sam thought it safe to get out and see what was going on.

Behind her, the front door to the house opened, and two more cowboy hats appeared, along with Kajsa and a woman with shoulder-length, dusty-brown hair. Sam felt like she'd just walked onto the set of an old western movie. She half expected John Wayne to come riding up on a horse and say, "Don't say it's a fine morning or I'll shoot ya."

The owner of a black hat jogged down the steps, barely flicking Sam a glance as he walked past. He had graying sideburns and frown wrinkles on the side of his mouth. "Colton McCoy, what have you done now?"

Sam eyed the driver of the truck with new interest. So that was the notorious rider of Maverick that Kajsa couldn't stop talking about. He turned his head to talk to the man wearing the black hat, who Sam assumed was his father, and she caught a glimpse of a handsome profile.

"I entered the wild mustang makeover contest," Colton said.

"You did *what*?" his father bellowed. His deep voice echoed off the mountain wall to the west of them.

Colton didn't seem too intimidated. "Wait until you see her. She's a beaut. Feisty as all get-out, but runs like the wind. I have one hundred days to train her. Think I can do it?"

"I'll tell you what I think you can do." His father jabbed a finger at the Chevy. "Get in the truck and take that animal back where it came from."

"Can't. It's all signed, sealed, and delivered," said Colton. "I was thinking we could keep her in the small corral next to the barn until she settles down."

"Son, how do you propose we pay for another horse? We can barely afford the ones we've got. And where are you going to find the time to train it? We've got the boarders to care for, the two quarter horses to train by July, and several riding lessons you're committed to teaching—not to mention all the upkeep of the ranch."

When Colton didn't reply, his father massaged his upper nose between his eyes and sighed. "What were you thinking, son?"

Colton shoved his hands into his pockets and considered the trailer. "I was thinking that horse can either sit in a federal holding facility the rest of its life, or I can find it a better home." He glanced at his father. "I'll make it work. I promise."

Another long sigh sounded, and the black hat shook, as though accepting the inevitable. "I suppose your brothers and I could help with the training of the quarter horses and some of the riding lessons."

"Speak for yourself, Dad," said a younger version of Colton, who still stood on the front porch. "Colt made his bed. I say we let him lay in it for a while."

His father's frown lines deepened. "And I say you've wasted enough time this morning as it is. Go get your brother, will ya? We have a wild horse to secure."

"Can I help?" piped up Kajsa, her eyes glowing with excitement.

Colton's father's expression softened as he looked down at her. "I'm going to have to say no to that one, darlin'. But you can watch from a distance."

"Is he like Maverick?" Kajsa breathed, watching the trailer with a mixture of awe and reverence.

Colton chuckled. "It's a *she*. And not yet, that's for sure. Though they do look alike."

"Can I see her?"

"In a few minutes," promised Colton. "I think we'd better let her calm down a little first."

Head still shaking, Colton's father patted Kajsa on the shoulder before grumbling to his wife, "He's your son."

"No. He's *our* son. And right now, I'm pretty proud of him."

Colton flicked a glance over his shoulder, and an attractive cleft formed in his chin as he smiled. His dark brown eyes held a tenderness that Sam immediately liked. "Thanks, Ma."

"Proud?" His father's voice boomed again. "Keeping every stray cat or puppy that finds its way onto our property is one thing. Adoptin' wild horses another." He pointed a finger at his son as he strode toward the barn. "This had better not become a habit."

Colton nodded, and his eyes finally landed on Sam. He gave her a quick once-over before approaching. "I'm sorry. Can I help you with something?"

Sam leaned her hip against her car and shook her head. "Just enjoying the family drama." *And the man who is causing said drama.*

Colton's mother laughed. "If drama's what you're after, feel free to drop by anytime. I have a feeling there will be plenty of that around here this summer." She sent her son a sharp glance before holding her hand out to Sam. "Forgive our rudeness, my dear. I'm Jane McCoy. This is our oldest son, Colton, and our favorite helper, Kajsa. The man with zero manners who just walked into the barn is my husband, Mike."

Sam took her hand and gave it a quick shake. "It's good to meet you. I'm—"

"She already knows me, Aunt Jane." Kajsa giggled. "That's Sam."

Recognition dawned on Mrs. McCoy's face. "Oh. I should have known. Kajsa talks about you so much that we feel like we already know you around here."

"You don't look much like a Sam," Colton said, moving to stand next to her. "I always pictured you burlier with facial hair and, uh . . . glasses." His close proximity made Sam's heart kick up a notch. Next to her short frame, he was tall and had a nice, earthy scent about him. A day or two of growth covered his face.

"Glasses?" Sam asked. How, exactly, had Kajsa described her?

The corner of his mouth twitched. "Kajsa said you were smart."

Sam met his direct gaze with one of her own. "Well, I'm smart enough to know that just because people shorten your name to Colt doesn't mean you have four legs, a long neck, or a tail."

He grinned. "Touché."

Mr. McCoy emerged from the barn, carrying a rope. At the same time, two slightly younger versions of Colton appeared from around the side of the house, looking like they'd just entered an arena to witness their first bull fight.

"Is it true, Colt?" called out the shorter one wearing a black cowboy hat. He still had that teenaged-lanky awkwardness about him, but his grin was almost as wide as his head was tall. "Did you really bring home a wild mustang?"

A loud whinny sounded from the trailer, followed by more banging. That horse definitely wanted out.

The two boys jogged up to the trailer and peered through the slats, laughing when they confirmed that there was, indeed, a wild animal inside.

"How do we get it out of there?" asked the taller of the two—the one who'd gone to fetch his brother earlier.

"By using you as bait," quipped Colton.

"Why me?" The taller elbowed the shorter. "Spence is the better choice. He used Mom's shampoo last night and still smells sweeter than—"

Spencer whacked him on the arm. "I wouldn't need to borrow hers if you'd stop using mine to wash the horses."

"But Mom's stuff smells so good on you." That earned the older brother another whack, which he quickly reciprocated.

"Stop it, you two," said Mr. McCoy. "What we're going to do is back the trailer up to the corral next to the barn and let the horse come out on its own."

Kajsa took a few quick steps in that direction before Colton caught hold of the back of her shirt. "Oh no, you don't. You're going to stay right here with . . ." He cast Sam an appreciative glance and winked. "Samantha."

It had been a long time since anyone had called her Samantha. The last time had been a professor on the first day of class, and Sam had quickly corrected her. She'd always preferred the short and sweet version of her name. It fit better, the way her yellow Bug fit her better than a Cadillac. But the way Samantha rolled off Colton's tongue had Sam reconsidering. Instead of sounding like a mouthful, her name became classy and feminine, like a classic-red Thunderbird convertible.

Maybe she'd been a little hasty to cross off "with a cowboy."

Sam took Kajsa's hand and waited next to Mrs. McCoy as the boys maneuvered the trailer around to the corral, secured the gates, and opened the back doors. A beautiful black horse burst into the corral, and the gate was quickly closed. The horse whinnied and slid into one fence after another, attempting to escape. She wore a dark green halter with a lead rope wrapped around her neck.

Kajsa pulled on Sam's hand, dragging her toward the corral. Sam's sandal scuffed against the dirt, and a prickly sticker wedged between two of her toes.

"One sec." Sam bent to remove it, and Kajsa ran to the men clustered around the corral, wedging herself between Colton and Mr. McCoy. Sam followed with Mrs. McCoy at a more sedate pace.

"I hope it's okay if I stay and watch for a little while," said Sam. "This is a lot more interesting than running errands."

Mrs. McCoy laughed. "You're welcome here anytime. The Mackies are family, which means you're family, so make yourself at home. If you'd like one of the boys to show you around, I have some boots you can borrow."

"I'll gladly take you up on that offer another time when you don't have so much going on."

Up ahead, Colton said something in Kajsa's ear and pointed, making her face glow with a happiness brighter than any of the trips to the lake or sidewalk chalk had ever done. Sam felt a moment's prick of jealousy before she replaced it with gratitude for Colton and his family. They'd welcomed Kajsa with open arms and hearts. Maybe they'd do the same for her.

"I think that's enough lollygagging for one day, boys," said Mr. McCoy. "It's time to get some work done around here. Dustin, why don't you get Marley out of the barn so we can start working with him, and Spence, you help Kajsa ready a new stall for the mustang."

"Can I watch a little longer?" begged Kajsa. "Please, Uncle Mike?"

His lips screwed to the side as he considered her plea. "I'll give you five more minutes. Any longer than that and we won't have time to do any riding today."

"Thank you!" She gave him a quick hug before climbing the fence to watch the horse.

Mr. McCoy stopped next to Sam on his way back to the barn, turning those frown lines on her. "And who might you be, young lady?"

"This is Sam," answered Mrs. McCoy.

"Ah," he said, as though needing no further explanation. He tipped his hat. "Welcome." Then he strode toward the barn without saying anything else. Evidently he was a man of few words.

"You really are welcome anytime," added Mrs. McCoy. "I have some stuff to do inside, but let me know if there's anything I can do for you."

"I will." Sam moved next to Kajsa, who was now standing on one of the rails in the fence, draping her little arms over the top as she stared at the mustang that was finally settling down. Sam leaned her shoulder against the fence and cocked her head at Colton.

"One hundred days, huh?" she asked.

"Yep."

"Ever trained a wild horse before?"

"Nope."

"How do you plan to do it?"

He flicked a glance her way before returning his attention to the horse. "Not sure yet. Guess I'll take it one day at a time and see what happens."

Sam laughed. "According to Kajsa you can do anything, so I'm sure you'll figure it out."

"That so, Kaj?" A hint of a smile appeared on Colton's mouth.

"You trained Maverick, didn't you?"

"Maverick was a baby. That's different than being raised in the wild."

Sam twisted around and rested her back against the fence, folding her arms as she looked over the property. The ranch-style house was older, but appeared in good condition.

The barn, on the other hand, had seen better days. The wood had aged to the point that it had buckled away from the posts in some places, leaving large gaps and holes. But against the backdrop of the mountains and shrubbery, it had an antique charm that a new building could never compete with. Sam decided she liked the barn just the way it was. She liked the ranch. And so far, she liked the family—especially one cowboy in particular.

"Watch out!" Kajsa jumped from the fence, and Sam glanced behind her to see the horse barreling toward her. Colton snagged her around the waist and jerked her away before the horse crashed into the fence where she'd just stood. A sharp pain pierced the heel of her right foot, causing her to latch on to Colton's arm to keep her balance.

"Oh, wow, that hurt." She tried not to grimace.

"You okay?" said Colton.

She tentatively put weight on her foot again, but quickly lifted it when she felt another stab of pain. "I think my heel slipped off my sandal and landed on something sharp. I'm pretty sure it's still in there." She let her sandal drop to the ground and lifted her foot to find a gnarly goat-head sticker jabbed in her heel. She quickly pulled it out and placed her thumb over the large drop of blood oozing from the hole.

"Kajsa, be a sweetheart and ask my mom for a Band Aid, will ya?" said Colton.

"I have one in the glove compartment in my car," said Sam.

Kajsa nodded and darted toward the car, leaving Sam still latched on to Colton's arm, feeling silly. "You must think I'm one of those high-maintenance girls who wears high heels to rodeos just so I can look pretty."

"The word 'prissy' never entered my mind," he said with a half smile.

Sam lifted her thumb from her heel. It still oozed a little blood, but she didn't care. She could clean her sandals later.

She dropped her foot and wriggled her toes back into her sandal. "I think I'm good now."

"You sure?"

"Yep." Time to go before she stepped on something else and embarrassed herself further.

Sam released his arm and hobbled across the dirt drive, her heel still throbbing like she'd been stung by a wasp. Kajsa was in the car, apparently still searching for the elusive first-aid kit. Sweet girl. Instead of oohing and ahhing over the new mustang, she was wasting her precious five minutes helping Sam.

"Will you be driving Kajsa every day?" asked Colton as he walked beside her.

Sam opened her door and said, "I'm okay, Kajsa," before turning back to Colton. "No. I'm just filling in while Cassie's gone. You'll see Sunshine the second come and go for the next two weeks and that's it. So enjoy my bright and happy car while you can."

"I like the touch of neon." He nodded toward her steering wheel.

"Me too," agreed Sam. "It's incredibly soft. You should get one for your truck."

"Thanks, but I'll pass. Is that a tennis ball over your gear shift?"

Sam nodded. "A souvenir from one of my roommates. We gave each other going away gifts at the end of the year. I got the steering wheel cover from the dancer, that ball from the tennis player, the charm from the jewelry designer, and a cute headband at home from the knitter, who also happens to be studying zoology—go figure. I'm just grateful she didn't give me a dead bug from her bug collection."

Colton leaned against her car and casually folded his arms. "What gift did you give?"

"A bottle of dish soap."

One of his dark eyebrows lifted in question. "Do you like washing dishes or something?"

"Hate it," said Sam. "One night I dragged all of them to the store, bought several bottles of dish soap, and sneakily dumped them into a fountain on the corner of an intersection. Within twenty minutes bubbles were everywhere, even crossing the street. From that point on I got nicknamed the bubble girl. Hence the dish soap. Plus we had a budget of only five dollars, so I didn't have too many options."

Colton chuckled and met her gaze with something resembling respect and interest. "So all the stories about you are true, huh?"

"What stories?" said Sam, trying to think of what tales the Mackies might have told.

Colton opened his mouth to say something when Kajsa's voice interrupted. "Sam, what does 'fling' mean?"

"Huh?"

"It's another way of saying throw," Colton answered. "Like I'm going to fling a rock at the fence or something like that."

A pause, and then, "How do you throw summer?"

Colton looked as confused as Sam felt. "What do you mean?"

Kajsa pointed to a notebook in her lap—*Sam's* notebook. The one containing her freshly written bucket list.

Oh no.

"This says, 'Have a summer fling.'"

At least she left out the "with a cowboy" part.

Sam leaned in to take the list away but whacked her shin against the frame of the car instead. She grabbed hold of her hurt leg, and in so doing, slammed her forehead against the top of the open car door before flopping down on the seat.

Unbelievable.

"Are you okay?" Kajsa asked.

"Fine." Now Sam's forehead, shin, and heel throbbed. She had the presence of mind to grab her notebook and flip it over on her lap.

"Easy there," Colton said, sounding like he was trying not to laugh. "This isn't how we like our guests to leave—covered in bumps, bruises, and puncture wounds."

In Sam's mind, the operative word had been leave—something she should have done fifteen minutes earlier, before the goat head, bruised shin, headache, and summer fling.

"Are you really going to ride a bull?" Kajsa asked, apparently not understanding the reason Sam took the notebook away.

"No," said Sam. *Stupid bucket list.* She no longer wanted to ride a horse, have a fling, or learn how to make lemon meringue either. All she wanted to do was shut the car door and drive away.

"What's a bucket list?" Kajsa was relentless.

"How about we talk about it later? I think your Uncle Mike is probably wondering what's taking you so long."

"Oh, right." That was all the reminder that Kajsa needed. She was out the door and gone in seconds, leaving the passenger door wide open.

Sam gingerly touched her tender forehead as she stared at the door, willing it to close on its own.

"Don't worry. I'll get that for you." Colton didn't give her a chance to argue. He quickly jogged around to the other side. Only instead of "getting" the door, he folded his tall body into Sam's little car without even the brim of his hat touching the frame.

How did he do that?

Her notebook was off her lap and in his hands before she had a chance to react.

Four

SAM LUNGED FOR the notebook, but Colton held it out of her reach. "A summer bucket list, huh?" he read, looking it over.

"Give that back."

"Hold your horses."

"I will not hold my horses." She continued to fight for her notebook. Who was this guy, anyway? She made a mental note to never let him anywhere near her journal.

"I've never made a bucket list before. This is interesting."

"*Now,* Colton."

He didn't obey. Instead he held it up, squinting against the morning sun as he continued to read. "Ride a horse, huh? I can give you a few lessons starting tomorrow if you want." He glanced at her, brow raised in question.

"What?" Sam stopped fighting and gaped at him instead. There was a gleam in his eyes that she couldn't figure out. A hint of tease with a dollop of cockiness, topped with sprinkles of sincerity.

"It says here you want to ride a horse before the summer's out, and I can make that happen. So? Do you want a few lessons or not? Tomorrow morning works for me."

Sam had no words. "Um . . . sure?"

"Great." He returned his gaze to the list. "You should move bull riding to the bottom."

"Why?"

"My father always says the only reason to ride a bull is to meet a nurse. Or a coffin. And from what I've seen, you don't need help finding excuses to meet nurses. And a coffin—well, you're still young."

Sam frowned. "I'm not typically so accident-prone."

But he'd already moved on and was squinting at the list again. "Have a summer fling." He paused. "It's a good thing you crossed off 'with a cowboy.'"

"Why?"

He raised an eyebrow as though he couldn't believe he had to explain. "Because cowboys don't have flings. It's all or nothing for us. For me, a fling would be like Kajsa first thought—throwing my summer away. What's the point of a fling, anyway?"

"I don't know. Something to put on a bucket list, I guess." *Something to put on a bucket list?* Sam groaned inwardly at herself. What was wrong with her? The purpose of a fling was to have a romantic adventure free from complications, entanglements, hurt feelings, and define-the-relationship talks. Simply put, it was for *fun*.

Why couldn't she have said that instead? Apparently a man who adopted wild horses, didn't do flings, and looked way too good in a cowboy hat had turned Sam's mind into a black hole.

At least "Something to put on a bucket list" was more than a one-word answer. She gave herself credit for that.

"*Run* a triathlon?" Colton had returned to her list. "Isn't biking and swimming involved as well? I mean, you can't exactly run in a pool or on a bike."

"Give me that." Sam reached for her list, only to be denied. Again.

"Skydiving?" He whistled. "Do you have a death wish or something?"

Sam dropped her head against the back of the headrest and folded her arms. "I like to think of it as an adventurous spirit."

"You're really prepared to jump out of a plane in the spirit of adventure?"

"Yes."

"What if your chute doesn't open?"

"I'll die a quick death and leave the rest of my bucket list to you in my will."

"Then it will probably remain unfinished, since apparently I don't have an adventurous spirit."

"You wouldn't jump out of a plane on my behalf?"

"I wouldn't jump out of a plane on anyone's behalf—not that I'd need to since you would have already done it."

Sam shifted positions, wishing she'd never written the stupid list. All she wanted to do was drive home and soak her body in a warm bath.

"You really want to learn to waltz?" he asked.

"What's wrong with that? As far as I know, nobody has ever died from waltzing."

"Nope, just the boredom of it."

"Can you please hurry and finish reading so I can leave?" she grumbled.

"Donate blood. I approve of that one."

"How kind."

"Create an ice sculpture?" He shook his head in a poor-naïve-you sort of way. "You know they use chainsaws to do that, right?"

Sam wasn't naïve, she didn't have a death wish, and if she wanted to make an ice sculpture, she would. "The bigger the chainsaw, the better."

He chuckled and returned to the list. "Learn how to make a to-die-for lemon meringue pie. That sounds good. I volunteer to be your taste-tester."

"Only if you agree to jump out of an airplane with me."

"Not happening."

"Then I'll ask Kajsa to taste-test for me. She'll probably be less critical anyway."

"It's called being honest." Back to the list. "See a moose in the wild. Find the perfect mascara. And . . . who the heck is Hugh Sheridan?"

"Only the most dreamy Australian actor/singer ever."

He nodded. "It's a good thing you crossed that off as well. Your chances of meeting him are probably about as good as surviving skydiving and bull riding."

"Gee thanks."

"Sleep under the stars—that's a good one. But dye your hair purple?" He shot her a look that said, *Are you insane?*

"Only for a week."

"But I like it blonde."

"I didn't ask what you liked."

"True." He finally handed the notebook back to Sam. His gaze rested on her face in a thoughtful, I'm-trying-to-figure-you-out-but-still-have-a-lot-of-questions way.

But he didn't ask any more questions. He simply tipped his hat. "Well, Samantha, it's been a pleasure. Guess I'll see you bright and early tomorrow morning." He pointed to her sandaled feet. "And I wouldn't wear those tomorrow if I were you."

"Yeah, figured that out on my own, thanks."

He grinned and slid out of the car in the same fluid way he'd gotten in and shut the door behind him. Sam twisted her key and started the engine, then watched him saunter back toward the wild mustang. Who was Colton McCoy exactly? Did she like him? Did she not like him? Did she want to take riding lessons from him, or did she want to offer to babysit the twins so Emma could be Kajsa's chauffeur for the next two weeks?

Sam honestly couldn't say.

Colton grinned at his garlic-laced mashed potatoes before shoving them into his mouth. Every time he thought of his encounter with Kajsa's treasured Samantha, he couldn't swipe the smile from his face. She'd turned out to be as gorgeous as she was interesting. Ride a bull? Have a fling? Jump out of a plane at fifteen thousand feet? Purple hair?

Had she written that list as a joke, or was she seriously planning to do those things? Thinking of that silky, curly blonde hair dyed purple made him snicker, and mashed potatoes shot into his air canal, making him cough and splutter and cough some more. He quickly chugged some water.

"What on earth is wrong with you?" asked his mother.

"Nothing." Colton returned his attention to his plate, trying to force his thoughts away from the image of spunk driving away in a yellow Bug called Sunshine II. Was there a Sunshine I?

"He's been acting that way ever since he met Kajsa's babysitter," taunted Dustin with one of his too-wide grins.

Colton suddenly felt the urge to press his brother's face into his potatoes.

"Her name's Samantha, and I'm giving her a few riding lessons. That's it," said Colton. They'd find out sooner or later, and he'd rather it be here, over dinner, than tomorrow morning when Samantha showed up to hear their reactions.

"You're doing *what*?" His father gaped at him from across the table.

"Teaching a couple of lessons. Not a big deal."

"Just like bringing home a wild mustang isn't a big deal?"

"I never said that wasn't a big deal. I only said I'd find a way to make it work."

"Just like you're going to make these extra lessons work?"

"That's right."

His father shook his head and frowned at his meal, looking ready to trade in his oldest son for someone with a lot more sense.

Colton's mother placed her hand over her husband's. "Oh, come now, Mike. I remember a time when you used to drive twenty minutes out of your way just to pick me up for school every day."

"That was different," he muttered.

"How so?"

"We were friends. He only met the girl this morning."

His wife smiled gently at him. "With as much as Kajsa and Adi talk about Sam, we've known her longer than that. Sometimes one meeting is all it takes."

This conversation was getting out of hand. Colton tossed his napkin onto his plate. "Takes for what? Good gravy, people. I'm not planning on marrying Samantha or even dating her. She expressed an interest in riding, and I offered to help. It's no different than what I did for Kajsa."

"You keep tellin' yourself that if it makes you feel better," said Dustin. "But you weren't coughing up mashed potatoes after you met Kajsa."

For whatever reason, the comment struck Spencer's funny bone, and he started cackling, spewing mashed potatoes of his own.

It was enough to make Colton's normally cool composure crack. More and more, he was ready to find his own place and put some distance between him and his family. He hadn't done it yet because the ranch meant everything to him, and despite his annoyance with his family, he loved them. Someday, this place would belong to him and his brothers, and Colton needed to learn all he could from his father before that day came.

But that was something he could still do while living under another roof.

"I've been thinking of moving into the shack," blurted Colton. He'd meant it as a joke, but as the idea settled in his mind, it turned into something that resembled an epiphany. Why hadn't he thought of that before?

Silence reigned in the room, all eyes trained on Colton. He gave himself a mental pat on the back for finding a way to shut his brothers up.

"Why would you want to do that?" his mother finally asked, her fork paused in the air halfway to her mouth.

"I'm twenty-six, Mom. It's long past time I lived on my own."

She set her fork down. And rested her chin on clasped knuckled. "But it's in horrible condition. I wouldn't let one of our cats live there."

Colton refrained from saying that the cats already spent a lot of time there—hunting mice. "I'm not talking about tomorrow. I'll fix it up first."

His father snickered and shook his head. "Son, you know there are only twenty-four hours in a day, right? Are you planning on getting any sleep this summer?"

At least his parents seemed to be considering it. "I can manage."

He gave a little scoff, as though giving up on reasoning with his son, and returned to his green beans.

"Can I have Colton's room when he's gone?" said Spencer, looking excited until his mother's glare had him dropping his gaze back to his plate.

A few awkward moments passed before his mother cleared her throat. "I suppose I can help you with the shack. If you're sure."

"I'm sure."

She nodded and looked down at her plate. Colton knew exactly what she was thinking. He could see it in her eyes and the telling expression on her face. She didn't like change, didn't like the thought of her oldest son moving out when there seemed to be no reason for him to do so.

But there was a good reason. Colton craved independence, change, and growth. He'd been ready to take that next step for a while now, but wanted to build a home of his own some day and couldn't justify the expense of renting an apartment when that extra money could go in a bank. And, like his mother said, the small cabin had always been a run-down, forgotten structure not fit for human habitation. But it had been years since anyone had been inside. Maybe it wasn't as bad as it looked. Maybe all it would need was a little TLC.

After rinsing his dishes and helping his mother clean up, Colton grabbed a flashlight and a notebook and headed up the lane, ready to make a list of his own. Only instead of riding bulls or jumping out of airplanes, his would include lots of to-dos.

Five

SAM TUGGED THE purplish curls into a ponytail and stared at the oval mirror hanging above her little white dressing table. After she'd left the McCoy's yesterday, she'd driven straight to Cal Ranch and purchased a hat, along with a sturdy-looking pair of cowboy boots. Then it was off to the grocery store for hair dye and her favorite treat—Andes mints. Colton had given her usual confidence a bit of a shake, and the dye was her way of firming it up again. She'd show him that his opinion didn't matter to her. The mints were merely food for thought.

Her parents had a dinner engagement, so Sam had invited Kajsa for a sleepover. They spent the evening listening to country music, learning a line dance from YouTube (so Sam could cross country dancing off her list), eating an entire half-gallon of mint chocolate chip ice cream (sprinkled with Andes mints), dying Sam's hair, and laughing hysterically at the results.

Take that, Colton McCoy, Sam had thought before crashing into bed and allowing a mint-induced coma to take over.

But now it was morning, and the daylight changed everything. The sun shone through the open window, highlighting Kajsa's shiny, beautiful brown hair as she brushed it into a cute ponytail. Sam's hair, on the other hand, looked more putrid than purple. Was this how people felt after spending the evening drinking and doing things they would never have done with an intact mind? Her stomach twisted and gurgled with the aftermath of the no-longer-yummy mints and ice cream.

She smashed her new tarnished-straw cowboy hat over her hair and frowned, realizing there was a reason her wardrobe didn't contain any purple items. It wasn't her color. She looked like a zombie trying to pass as a cowgirl.

She forced her lips into a smile. "Ready to go, Kajsa?"

The darling girl giggled when she looked at Sam. "Your hair looks awesome."

Liar, Sam thought. "Maybe tonight we can dye yours to match."

The shiny, brown ponytail shook with Kajsa's head. "No, that's okay," which was Kajsa's kind way of saying that awesome really meant hideous.

Sam grabbed Kasja's brown hat and set it gently on her head. "Let us away then, my dear. The day isn't getting any younger."

"Huh?"

"Never mind." Sam hunted through her purse, looking for her phone and her keys. Maybe she should take Kajsa out for breakfast. That way they could get out of the house before her mother woke up and discovered—

"What on earth have you done to your hair?"

So much for that plan. Sam blew a purple curl from her face and turned around to face her mom, wondering if the sun catcher her roommate had given her was actually bad luck.

"She dyed it," said Kajsa.

"I can see that." Her mother walked into the room and

lifted the hat from Sam's head. She didn't bother trying to hide a grimace. "May I ask why?"

Sam played it cool. "I had no choice. It was on my bucket list."

"She has to have a fling with summer and ride a bull too," inserted Kajsa.

"What?"

Oh brother, Sam thought. She stole the hat back from her mom and pressed it down over her hair, brushing all loose strands behind her ears. "It's not like I'm planning to follow through with everything on the list."

"Just like you didn't follow through with dying your hair purple?" said her mom.

"I was high on Andes mints at the time. You know I can't be responsible for my actions when that happens."

Her mother rolled her eyes. "Sometimes you are too impulsive for your own good."

"I'm definitely feeling it this morning, yes."

"Thank goodness you have more sense, Kajsa." Her mom smoothed Kajsa's ponytail with an expression that said, *I wish my daughter's hair looked as good as yours.* With a sigh, she put her arms around both girls. "C'mon. I have some hot-off-the-grill waffles for you downstairs. They should taste good, even though they're the same old boring neutral color they usually are. Maybe I should have added some purple food coloring."

"Don't even start, Mom."

"Oh, I haven't begun to start. Just wait until your father sees you."

Sam didn't have to wait long. Her father was already in the kitchen, digging into a stack of waffles covered in berries. With resignation, Sam lifted the hat from her head and pointed to her hair. "You have five seconds. Go."

He blinked at her.

"Five, four, three-two-one. Time's up."

He nodded and returned to his waffles.

With her hands on her hips, her mother shook her head. "Justin, I'm disappointed. You had the perfect opportunity to give our daughter some sage advice, and you blew it."

"I'm pretty sure she's learned her lesson," came his reply.

Sam couldn't agree more. Learned her lesson and would continue to learn it. What would Colton say when he saw it? Sam didn't want to even think about it. She piled two plates high with waffles, drizzled a heavy helping of syrup over the top of each, and handed one to Kajsa. Then she took a seat next to her father. "I'm thinking next time I should color it green. What do you think?"

"Sort of like how your hair looked that summer after you made the swim team?" he asked.

He made a good point. "You're right. Blonde it is."

"My favorite look on you."

Kajsa only ate half her waffle before dragging Sam out the door, saying she couldn't wait to see the mustang any longer. The two girls sped off in a flurry of purple, brown, and yellow, arriving at the McCoy ranch a little earlier than planned.

They found Colton in the small corral next to the barn, holding the mustang's lead rope and letting the animal run circles around him. Colton stood in the middle, spinning slower circles in a patient, lackadaisical way, almost as though the movements of the horse had hypnotized him. He wore a blue and gray flannel shirt.

Kajsa scrambled up the fence and rested her elbows on the top rail, watching the horse with rapt attention. Sam stayed back a few feet, more leery of the wild animal after it had charged her yesterday.

"What's her name?" Kajsa asked.

Colton glanced at Kajsa before his gaze settled on Sam. "Nice hat."

"Thanks." She'd pulled her hair into a ponytail and

looked at him straight-on, trying to keep the purple hidden for as long as possible. "Where's the rest of your family?"

"Mom had to run a few errands, and Dad took my brothers to Denver to get a load of feed."

"All the way to Denver?" asked Sam.

"We get it cheaper from a supplier up there, so we always stock up. That way we only need to make the trip every few months."

"So?" prodded Kajsa, more interested in the horse than the feed. "Does she have a name yet?"

Colton continued to turn with the animal, his movements slow and methodical, but his attention remained on the girls. "I don't know yet. I was actually thinking of letting you figure it out, Kaj."

"Really?"

"It has to be a good name—one fitting of a beautiful animal with a wild heart and an intelligent mind."

Kajsa bit her bottom lip and cast a worried glance Sam's way, as though the responsibility of the job was more than she wanted to take on.

"You'll figure out the perfect name," Sam encouraged, taking a few steps closer. "Just make sure you don't take too long deciding. Everyone needs a name."

"What would you name her?" Kajsa asked.

Sam leaned her shoulder against the fence, facing Kajsa, and gave it some thought. What did people name horses, anyway? Black Beauty, Mr. Ed, Maximus, Whisper, and Maverick were the only ones she could think of. Apparently, they could be named pretty much anything.

"Pineapple?" offered Sam as a suggestion.

Kajsa doubled over in laughter. "She would buck you off if you ever called her that. Pineapple doesn't fit her at all."

Apparently you couldn't name a horse anything. The name had to fit. But fit what? Personality? Appearance? Nature? "I'm pretty sure she'd buck me off no matter what I called her," said Sam.

"She's a leader, so it has to be a leader name. Like . . ." Kajsa's voice trailed off, and a thoughtful frown replaced her smile.

"Commander in Chief?" Sam joked. "George Washington? What about just Washington?" She actually liked that one, but Kajsa was shaking her head.

A loud whinny, followed by snorting, came from the corral. "What's wrong with you now?" said Colton as the horse pranced in place as though anxious about something.

Ever so slowly, Sam stepped away from the fence and tensed, ready to grab Kajsa if the horse came charging again. "I don't think she likes me much."

Colton gave the horse a considering look. "Why would you say that?"

"She was doing fine until I showed up. And yesterday she charged me. Just look at her. I swear she's glaring at me."

Kajsa giggled. "It sort of looks like she is."

Colton shook his head in a give-me-a-break sort of way. "She's a wild horse that doesn't like being confined in a corral. It has nothing to do with you."

"She's not charging you."

"Only because I spent all of yesterday afternoon with her." Colton tugged lightly on the lead rope, trying to encourage the horse to move forward again, but it wasn't until Kajsa said, "You can do it, girl," that she finally did.

Colton could say all he wanted about wild horses, but Sam knew that horse had something against her. But what? Maybe horses really could sense fear and didn't like cowards.

"Is this part of the training process?" Sam asked.

"Yeah," answered Colton. "Right now she trusts me enough to let me inside the corral, but that's it. I need her to stop running and come to me on her own—let me touch her."

"She won't let you touch her?" Kajsa asked.

"Haven't really tried. She let me unhook her lead rope

after I fed her a carrot, but that's it. I don't want to force a connection. When she's ready, she'll come."

Sam continued to watch the horse canter, feeling a little hypnotized herself. How long had Colton been at this? How was he not dying of boredom? Sam had only been here ten minutes and already needed a change of pace.

"Kajsa, don't you have work to do?" Colton cocked his head at her and smiled.

"Five more minutes, please?"

"Tell you what. Get all your chores done first thing every day, and I'll let you help me train the mustang."

Eyes wide and excited, Kajsa leapt from the fence and raced toward the barn, not giving Colton a chance to rescind his offer.

"I will be checking to make sure you do a good job," Colton called after her.

"I will," was the last they heard before she disappeared inside.

Colton pointed a gloved finger at Sam. "Now *that* is the proper way to motivate someone."

"Bribery?"

"Incentives."

"In that case, what will be my 'incentive' for learning how to ride?" she said.

"When you can take off on a horse without fear, feeling the wind on your face and the power beneath you, you'll have your reward."

Colton slowed his movements, tugging lightly on the rope to encourage the mustang to stop. He spoke in a low voice as he cautiously approached the animal. "I'm going to remove this rope from your halter, if that's okay." Her head bobbed up and down, but she allowed him to unclip the rope before trotting to the other side of the corral, near a gate that led to the pasture containing the other horses. She nudged the gate with her long nose and Colton laughed.

"Not yet. You have to show me you can trust me first."

He swung over the fence and was at Sam's side a moment later, removing his work gloves.

"You ready for—" He stopped and took a closer look at Sam then lifted the end of her ponytail and fingered the curls, sending a rippling sensation down her back. Sam steeled herself for what was to come. But instead of the expected snarky remark, he dropped her hair and looked into her eyes. "I can see you're serious about that bucket list."

"I am," she said, though she planned to replace *Ride a bull* with *Win a stuffed giraffe at the county fair*.

"In that case, let's get you on a horse."

He started for the barn, and Sam had to speed-walk to keep up. "Really? That's it? No jokes about me looking like I'm trying to pass for NYU's mascot?"

"I'm pretty sure NYU already has a mascot."

They entered the barn, and strong odors of leather, hay, and manure permeated everything. Kajsa was scooping up hay with a pitchfork and transferring it to the last stall on the left, while a medium-sized chestnut horse occupied the first stall on the right.

Colton grabbed a bridle hanging from a peg on the wall. "What do you think, Kaj? Will Samantha do all right with Nutmeg?"

Kajsa rested her cheek against the handle of the pitchfork and considered the question. "Yeah, I think Nutmeg's a good choice," she said before returning to her work.

"I agree." Colton flashed a grin and lowered his voice so only Sam could hear. "I love that girl."

For a brief moment, Sam wished she was a cowgirl at heart instead of just dressed like one.

"Hey, you got boots too." Colton nodded at her new footwear.

"If I'm going to learn to ride a horse, I'm going to do it right."

"Are you going to invest in chaps too, for when you ride that bull?"

"Chaps, gargantuan belt buckle, spurs, you name it," said Sam. "I never do anything halfway."

The sound of his chuckle echoed off the walls of the barn, filling the space with richness and depth. It made her wonder what a full-blown laugh would sound like. Probably really good. The kind of laugh that would make people stop, stare, and hope for more.

Sam mentally added another item to her bucket list: Make Colton really laugh.

"Have you ever ridden a bull?" she asked as he fitted the bridle on Nutmeg.

"Once." He led the horse from the stall and handed the reins to Sam. "Hold her steady while I get her saddled."

It was a little unnerving standing in front of an animal with a mass at least three times her size, but Sam forced her fingers to tighten around the straps as she tried not to tense or show fear. Nutmeg shuffled his hooves, and Sam shuffled her boots.

"Is Nutmeg a he or a she?" Sam asked.

"*She's* Maverick's girlfriend." Colton yanked on a strap, tightening it around the belly of the beast. "Maverick's my horse."

"Yeah, I've heard all about him from Kajsa." Sam lowered her voice. "She idolizes both of you, and frankly I'm a little jealous. I feel like I've been replaced."

Colton finished tying off the strap before he dropped the stirrup. "Trust me when I say that you are still number one in her eyes. I could never compete with How to Host a Murder parties, tie-dying t-shirts to look like rainbows, or making water rockets." He gave Nutmeg a quick rub on the neck. "Yesterday, when my mom said we feel like we already know you, it's because we kind of do. Between Kajsa and the rest of her family, I've lost count with how many times your name pops up in conversations. Kajsa may love horses, but she adores you."

As Colton spoke, a warmth radiated from Sam's chest through the rest of her body, making her feel like one of those Glo Worms she used to sleep with as a kid. Sam knew she could never compete with Colton or Maverick or horses in general, but maybe she didn't have to. Maybe it was like one of those delicious, layered desserts. Kajsa's family was the crust that held everything together, this ranch was the yummy pudding layer, and Sam the fluffy whipped cream on top. And that was okay. Everyone's life was layered. It was in the combining of the individual layers that turned a tasty life into something decadent.

Sam held out the reins, hoping Colton would take them back, which he did. "You said you rode a bull once. What's the story there?"

He cracked a smile as he led the horse from the barn. "It was an amateur rodeo, and some of my friends who'd signed up for bull riding pressured me into doing the same. My parents thought I'd lost my marbles, but what teenaged kid listens to his parents, right? I mean, that wouldn't be cool, and a certain girl I wanted to impress was planning to be there. So I signed up, cinched my hand to the back of a bull named Dominator, and made it two seconds before I was thrown against a fence. I managed to break both arms, and for six weeks, my right arm was in a full cast, from my shoulder to my hand, and my left from my elbow to my hand. It didn't take long for the coolness factor to wear off and for me to come to my senses. And the nurse who helped fix me up was a man."

Sam laughed. "But you still train horses, and I'm guessing you get bucked off a lot doing that."

"I do, and I've gotten a few more broken bones in the process. But it's different when you're doing something dangerous for a positive outcome instead of for sport. There's nothing more rewarding than gaining a horse's trust, figuring him out, and teaching his owner to do the same. In my world, a horse that can't be trained is ultimately a dead horse, so I do everything in my power to keep that from happening. And when I win, which I usually do, it feels pretty great."

As Colton led Nutmeg through a gate and into a large pasture, Sam thought about what he'd said and wondered even more about layers and people. What made Colton Colton? He was handsome and grinned more times than he didn't, but he was also nosy and snarky, with a confidence bordering on cockiness. And yet he'd taken a little girl under his wing, adopted a wild mustang to save it from a sad fate, and offered a few riding lessons so a girl could cross something off her bucket list.

Like most people, Colton was layered. But when all those layers came together, was he more like a rainbow Jello salad that looked better than it tasted, or was he more like a luscious berry trifle with color and flavor and a taste that made Sam's mouth water just thinking about it?

Yesterday, Sam wasn't sure she wanted to come back to the McCoy ranch, but now she wanted to stay, learn, and uncover all the layers of all the people in the McCoy family—especially Colton.

"Hold your hand under her nose like this so she can get used to your smell," Colton said, showing her what he meant.

Sam did as he asked, praying Nutmeg wouldn't open that large mouth and chomp down on her fingers. But the horse only sniffed and brushed her surprisingly soft nostrils against the back of Sam's hand.

"Now rub her gently right here and say something nice," Colton said in Sam's ear, guiding her hand to Nutmeg's neck. A flurry of warmth and chills flooded up her arm and into her body, making her want to lean into Colton. Did he really expect her to say something intelligent to a horse when all she could think about was his breath on her neck or his hand touching hers?

"Say, 'Hi, Nutmeg,'" Colton coached when Sam didn't say anything.

More chills. More warmth. "Hi, Nutmeg."

"My name's Samantha."

"My name's Sam."

"When I ride you," he continued.

"When I ride you," came her echo.

"I want you to run faster than you've ever run before."

"I want you to—whoa, what?" Sam pulled her hand free and backed away from Colton in an attempt to unfog her brain. "What kind of sorry excuse for a teacher are you? I don't want Nutmeg to run. I want her to walk. Slowly. Like a turtle."

And then it came. His real laugh. A hearty sound that stretched across the field, over the hills, and into the valleys, filling, spreading, encompassing until it had wrapped around her in a tight embrace as though saying, *I think you're something special.*

It was a silly way to feel because he was laughing *at* her, not *with* her. People didn't laugh at special things. They laughed at silly, ignorant, foolish things.

"All right, Nutmeg. You heard the lady. Let's take it slow." He chuckled again and interlaced his fingers to create a make-shift step then nodded toward the saddle. "Up you go."

"What, now? Already?" Sam glanced around the pasture. Several unleashed horses grazed in the distance with no fence or natural barrier between her and them. At any moment, they could stop eating and decide to play a game of tag with Nutmeg. Was Colton really planning to teach her here?

Apparently so. Apparently he was a jump-in-with-both-feet type of teacher.

"But I don't even know how to control her." No way

would Sam sit on any horse, even one as sweet as Nutmeg seemed, without a crash course in how to use the reins.

"You don't control a horse. You work *with* her."

"And how do I do that?"

"I'll show you. Once you're in the saddle." With his fingers still clasped, he nodded toward the horse.

Sam sighed and lifted her right boot.

"Other foot."

Oh, right. She switched feet and grabbed hold of the saddle horn. Colton tossed her onto the horse like she was a flyweight. She settled into the saddle and took the reins from him, keeping a firm grip on the horn, while Colton took the horse by the bridle.

"Okay, so the first thing you need to know is—" He stopped abruptly and squinted at something behind her—something that sounded like pounding hooves. "How the heck did she get out?" he muttered under his breath.

Sam twisted in the saddle and froze when she saw a large black horse stirring up the dirt as it ran toward them. It was the nameless, wild mustang that that seemed to like Sam about as much as it liked fences. Nutmeg started to back up, pulling against the hold Colton had on her bridle.

"Easy there, girl. Just stay put." Much to Sam's horror, Colton let go of Nutmeg's rope and moved to stand between the wild horse and Sam, holding out his hand as though the gesture would somehow keep the wild horse from taking him down.

"Colton, move!" Sam yelled, sickened at the thought of what was about to happen. What should she do? What *could* she do? Why wasn't Colton moving? Why wasn't that stupid wild animal slowing down?

And then Nutmeg bolted.

Six

SAM DROPPED THE reins and grabbed the saddle horn with both hands, holding on as tight as she could. Her beautiful hat flew off her head, yanking several strands of hair with it, and her body thumped against the saddle, bouncing like a ping pong ball against the rhythm of the horse. Her muscles stretched and strained to hold on as she struggled to get her body to move with Nutmeg's. Eventually, she got the feel of it and was finally able to glance back.

Colton was nowhere in sight and that horrible black horse was gaining on them. What would happen when it caught up? Would it bite down on Sam's leg, rip her from Nutmeg's back and trample her to death? Was that how this was going to end?

About one hundred feet ahead, a wooden fence stretched across the field, perpendicular to them. Instead of changing directions, Nutmeg increased her speed, racing toward the fence as though she meant to jump it. Fear seized Sam's heart, and she had the crazy thought that if she died, she'd be put to rest for all eternity with putrid, purple hair.

She ducked her head, clutched the horn with all the strength she had left, and squeezed the saddle between her legs.

The horse's hooves left the ground, and Nutmeg sailed up and over what Sam assumed was the fence. When they reconnected with solid ground, the force tore her fingers from the horn, and she flew off the back of the horse. Her shoulder hit the ground first—or maybe it was a rock—followed by the rest of her body. She lay in a daze for a moment before lifting her aching head and looking around for the crazed mustang. It strutted around behind the fence, as though attempted murder was something to be proud of.

Something inside of Sam snapped. She struggled to her feet and limped forward, letting her anger overshadow her pain. "What is wrong with you?" she screamed at the horse. "I've done nothing to you. Nothing! Was I the one who captured you? No! Was I the one who brought you here? No! Am I the one trying to tame you into submission? No! I only came to bring Kajsa and ride a nice horse. I want nothing to do with you. Nothing! So do me a favor and *leave me alone!*" She was at the fence now, gripping it hard and screaming so loud it made her throat raw.

The mustang sniffed, scuffed the ground with its two front hooves, then cantered away, leaving Sam fuming. When the horse was finally out of sight, Sam turned around to find that Nutmeg was nowhere to be seen either.

Awesome. Her beautiful straw hat was no more, the color of her body now matched her hair, and her throat hurt from screaming at a horse. She sank down to the ground and leaned her aching back against a wooden post. In only a few short days, she'd gone from being an enthusiastic graduate with a bright future ahead of her to someone who belonged in the psych ward. Her summer was cursed, and that's all there was to it.

The four-wheeler buzzed beneath Colton, refusing to go any faster. He stood on the machine, absorbing every bump and obstacle with his legs as he surged in the direction the horses had run. He cursed himself for ever taking Sam into the field and putting her on the horse. But mostly, he cursed himself for entering that stupid mustang makeover contest.

First thing tomorrow, that horse was going back where it came from.

On the other side of the fence, Colton spied a riderless Nutmeg cantering down the road. He sped toward the fence and slammed his foot into the emergency brake at the same time he squeezed the handlebars. The machine slid to the side and skidded to a stop, and Colton was off it and over the fence in seconds. He ran to Nutmeg, spoke softly to calm her down, then jumped on her back. "Take me to Samantha, girl."

Colton had worked with horses his entire life. He'd been bitten, kicked, stepped on, charged, and thrown. But he'd never felt true fear because of any horse until now. Where was Samantha? What had happened to her? Had she fallen off before or after Nutmeg jumped the fence?

"Samantha!" he shouted. "Where are you?"

No answer.

He continued cantering along the road, calling out her name over and over again. Finally, he heard a weak reply.

"I'm here," she called.

Colton let out a breath of relief and directed Nutmeg off the road, toward her voice. He found her sitting next to a fence, with her arms wrapped around her bent, denim-clad legs. Her purple curls looked wild and untamed, and her face was streaked with dirt.

He swung down from Nutmeg and jogged to her side, squatting down beside her. "You okay?" he said, brushing her hair away from her face.

"I told you that horse hates me."

At least her sense of humor was still intact. There were

no tears in those beautiful green eyes either. Only frustration. And possibly embarrassment. Colton held out a hand. "Can you walk?"

She ignored him, saying glumly, "My hat is gone, my hair is purple, and I smell like dirt and maybe something worse."

"I found your hat, the smell will wash off, and the purple is growing on me."

"Liar," she said. But at least the corners of her mouth no longer drooped.

Colton placed his hands under her elbows and gently lifted her up.

"Ow," she complained as she stood.

He touched her shoulders lightly. "Are you sure you're okay?"

"Not broken. Just bruised."

Colton wondered if she'd ever want to ride again. Probably not. He hated himself because of it.

She shook her head when he led her back to Nutmeg. "I know if you fall off, you're supposed to get right back on, but I really don't want to."

"It's a long walk with a bruised body." A *beautiful* bruised body that curved in all the right places. Even with her wild, purple hair, Samantha was still easy on the eyes.

She blew some air from the corner of her mouth and sighed. "Okay."

"We'll go slow. I promise." He eased her up on the horse then swung up behind her, holding her trim body between his arms. He picked up the reins and urged Nutmeg into a nice and easy walk. After a few strides, Sam relaxed her back against Colton's chest. She felt soft and good, and he noticed that her hair didn't smell like dirt. It smelled like mangos and pineapple and coconut.

"Is this how you teach all your clients to ride?" Sam said. "Toss them on a horse with no instruction and release the wild mustang?"

A snicker escaped his lips. The things that came out of her mouth sometimes. "No. I reserve that treatment for only the special clients—the tough ones I know can take it."

"You pegged me wrong."

"I don't think so. You got back on the horse, didn't you?"

"Only because I didn't want to hoof it back, no pun intended."

Even after all she'd been through, Samantha still had a healthy dose of spunk. Colton appreciated that. "If it makes you feel any better, I'll be taking the mustang back first thing tomorrow."

"Why?" She tried to twist to look at him, but her face pulled into a grimace of pain, and she quickly turned back.

"That's why," Colton answered, his jaw clenched tight.

"But Kajsa—"

"Will understand." After today's episode, Samantha would probably crawl into that yellow Bug and speed out of here as fast as she could. There would be no more riding lessons, no more wild, purple hair or toned legs, and no more unexpected comments that would make him laugh like he hadn't laughed in a long time.

Colton hadn't exaggerated about all the stories he'd heard about Samantha. They had piqued his curiosity. He'd always wanted to meet the girl who'd strung a clothesline between her house and the one across the street, creating a make-believe world where two young girls became secret agents, charged with decoding mysterious secret messages that would come in through the window. The girl who'd buried Kajsa's cut-off hair in the garden after Adi had cut it too short, promising that planting it would make Kajsa's hair grow faster. The girl who built snow caves and painted them to look like fairy houses.

Even before Colton had actually met Samantha, she'd inspired him. And now that all those stories had been personified in a living and breathing, beautiful body, Colton was reluctant to let her slip away. Maybe it was selfish, but he didn't want to just hear about those stories, he wanted to be in them.

"What's that?" Samantha took the reins from Colton and pulled on them to make Nutmeg stop and pointed to a run-down little log cabin, set back about fifty yards from the road.

"We call it The Shack," Colton said. "I'm in the process of fixing it up so I can move in." Not that he'd gotten very far. Colton had spent a few hours there the previous evening, mostly filling up garbage bags and setting out mouse traps.

"You're serious."

"Yep."

"That is so cool." He could hear the smile in her voice. "Can I see it?"

"Um . . ." Colton thought about the warped wooden floor, the dust-and-cobweb covered windows, and all the dead mice or rats that were undoubtedly "lounging" around. Even dirty and purple-haired, Samantha didn't belong in that cabin. Not yet anyway.

"Oh, come on," she said, pulling on his hands to try and steer Nutmeg toward it. "It has an aura of mystery and neglect—a place where old and interesting stories hang out."

"And spiders," added Colton.

"Spiders?" Her fingers stiffened over his, and Colton smiled.

"Big, hairy, spiders. They look like tarantulas on steroids with fangs." Okay, so maybe that was a little overkill because she was yanking on the reins again, apparently not buying any of it.

"Not that way, Nutmeg. This way."

With a sigh, Colton fed the reins through her fingers and showed her how to gently guide the horse to the right. Nutmeg followed immediately.

"I would have known how to do that if you'd taught me some of the basics," Samantha said.

"Yeah, yeah."

They stopped in front of the house, and Colton slid off the horse, then carefully helped Samantha down. She immediately walked to the door and tried to open it, but it wouldn't budge.

"Is it locked?"

"Sort of." Colton slammed his shoulder into the wood, and it flew open with a loud creak. Everything about this place either creaked or squeaked. It was old. Very, very old.

Samantha grinned. "So that's how you lock doors around here."

Colton eyed a nasty, flattened mouse in a nearby trap. "Unfortunately, it doesn't keep the critters out."

"Okay, that's gross." She had a stronger stomach than he'd expected because the sight of all the dead rodents didn't keep her from wandering through the tiny cottage. She crossed the creaky floor, opened the squeaky bedroom door, and looked inside. A queen-sized bed was covered with a worn and dusty patchwork quilt that Colton's grandmother had made. Two simple nightstands flanked each side, leaving the rest of the room barren.

"Quaint," Sam said before moving on.

The bathroom door was already open, revealing a stained, yellow tub, a toilet, and a small vanity. An ancient stacked washer and dryer unit sat in the corner.

"No shower?" she asked.

"That's going to be one of the improvements I make after I move in. I don't like baths."

"After a day like today, a hot bath sounds heavenly," said Samantha. "But I couldn't live without a shower either."

She peeked in a small storage closet next, opened a few of the knotty pine kitchen cupboards, ran her fingers across the time-distressed wooden table, and finally looked Colton's way.

"It's charming," she announced. "Or, at least it will be once you fix it up."

"You think?" They must be looking through different colored glasses, because all Colton could see were the dead critters, cobwebs and problems.

"Yeah." She glanced around again. "I could help, if you want."

His eyes snapped to hers. Did she really just offer to not go away? To do something with him that could turn into a story?

"I do want," he said quickly. "I mean, if you're sure you have the time, I would love some help."

She waved off his concern. "I've got the whole summer to kill. My job doesn't start until the fall."

Colton liked the sound of that—spending the entire summer with her, that is. "What job is that?"

"A junior graphic designer," she answered. "I'll be creating everything from images for t-shirts to CD labels, advertisements, invitations, and brochures. I can't wait."

That career choice seemed to fit her perfectly. Creative, interesting, and fun.

She sat down on one of the two wooden dining chairs and smiled when it squeaked and swayed under her lightweight frame. "I think you could use some new furniture."

"Nah, I could never get rid of this stuff." He wiggled the other chair and decided it would be safer to remain standing. "This house was built by my great-great-grandfather nearly one hundred years ago. He purchased the land from the government when Colorado Springs was nothing more than a baby. Together, with my great-great grandmother, they lived here for about five years while they got the ranch going. Then they built a larger home down the road where ours now stands. Forty years ago, my grandfather grew tired of living in a home with endless problems, but he liked the location, so he leveled the old house and built a new one in its place—where my family lives now. This house, on the other hand, still has the same walls and most of the original furniture."

Colton looked around him, feeling the pride that came from a long legacy of hard-working family members who had labored to make something lasting out of nothing. Even though they called this place The Shack, Colton didn't smell the must or rotted wood. He smelled history and a really good place to call home. "When my parents first married, they modernized it with indoor plumbing and electricity and added on that bathroom and laundry area. They lived here until they had me, then moved into the big house to take care of my grandparents before they passed."

Sam's finger followed the grain lines on the table, rising and falling with the waves of the distressed, warped wood. "Is that what you're planning to do? Live here until you're ready to move back to the big house and take over?"

Between Colton and his brothers, one of them was expected to carry on the McCoy legacy, but for Colton, instead of feeling like a no-way-out responsibility, it felt like a privilege—the grand prize for being born a McCoy and learning what it meant to work hard. Ranching was in his blood, just like the property and houses were in his blood. Nothing could change that. He didn't want anything to change that.

"I plan to eventually take over, but I don't want to move back into the big house. We have a lot of property here, and I'd prefer to build my own place someday." At least that's what Colton hoped would happen. But maybe it wouldn't. Maybe he'd never marry or have a family of his own. Maybe he'd stay here, in this shack, for a good long while. Who knew what life held in store for him? He'd worry about it when the time came.

Samantha nodded. Then her gaze drifted out the tiny kitchen window, to where Nutmeg stood grazing. Her brow furrowed. "Why did Nutmeg jump the fence but the mustang didn't?"

Colton held out his hand and pulled her up, leading her out of the house. He yanked the door closed behind him and said, "Back in the day, Nutmeg was a jumper—a really good one—until she tore a major tendon. That kind of injury takes a year or more to heal, and Nutmeg was close to retirement anyway, so the owners cut their losses and sold her to us. Now she's one of the best riding horses we have. But that doesn't mean she's given up her jumping days. Every once in a while we find her outside the pasture, trotting down the road like she owns the place." He smiled as he helped her on the horse, noticing she didn't wince as much this time.

"She's definitely earned my allegiance," said Samantha. "Though I'd rather not be riding her the next time she decides to relive her glory days."

Colton swung up behind her and guided Nutmeg back toward the road. "Your hat is back on my four-wheeler. Other than a little dirt, it's still good as new."

"Thank you," she said. "I'm going to need it a lot during the next seven days to cover up this beautiful hair of mine."

"You can always cross off the part about keeping it purple for a week."

"I will not," said Samantha. "What's the point of having a bucket list if I'm allowed to revise it?"

"You revised the part about having a fling with a cowboy."

"That was before I finished the list. Now that it's finished, it's set in stone."

Colton nodded, not liking the idea of her dating someone else. Maybe he'd been too hasty in saying he didn't do flings.

Wait, what was he thinking? Not only were flings a waste of time, but they created awkward messes in the future. They weren't worth the long-term consequences no matter how fun or gorgeous the girl. Colton wanted a relationship with the potential to go beyond summer and into the rest of his life. He wanted someone who would be happy settling down with him on this ranch in that poor excuse for a cabin and find the lifestyle as invigorating as he did.

Samantha Kinsey would never be happy here. Would she? Who was she, really? What sort of life did she see herself living? She came across as the type of person who bounced from one adventure to the next, refusing to put down any roots. The type of person who was okay with dyeing her hair purple, sculpting ice, and having flings because it was all temporary.

Maybe she feared permanence.

The house came into sight, and moments later, Samantha's body stiffened between his arms. Colton followed her gaze out to the pasture and gripped the reins hard. His first instinct was to yell out Kajsa's name and spur Nutmeg into a run, but Sam's gentle touch on his arm kept him quiet and steady.

"Wait," she whispered.

Seven

GROWING UP ON a ranch, Colton had experienced many things he considered to be sacred. Like the day he'd helped bring his first foal into the world, the time he'd known just where to find Spencer, who'd gotten lost in the mountains during an overnight camping trip, and the awe he felt every time he rode high into the mountains and looked over what had become of the Colorado Springs valley.

Colton was no stranger to miracles. So when he saw the wild mustang nuzzling Kajsa's cheek and allowing her to stroke its jaw, he knew he was witnessing something extraordinary.

Kajsa ducked under the mustang's neck to rub its shoulder then giggled when the horse's nose tickled her back. If Colton didn't know any better, he would think the beautiful black horse was tame and gentle—the kind of animal he'd let a toddler ride. But it hadn't been tamed or gentled. It had just charged Samantha and Nutmeg, and only yesterday it had tried to tear apart the trailer and take down the corral fence.

Colton tensed, half expecting the mustang to rear back and do the whole Jekyll/Hyde thing again, but she only nuzzled, sniffed, and stood there. He would have spurred Nutmeg on anyway if he wasn't worried about upsetting the mustang again.

"Look at them," whispered Sam. "You can't take that horse back tomorrow."

Colton didn't know what to think. Would the horse continue to run down some people then turn around and play Mr. Docile to Kajsa? It was crazy.

Eventually, Kajsa grabbed hold of the halter and led the mustang through the wide open gate and into the corral, which made Colton wonder how the animal had gotten out in the first place.

As Kajsa locked the gate, the horse lifted its head, looking in the direction of Samantha and Colton then turned and began trotting around the corral as though nothing out of the ordinary had happened.

"At least she didn't charge you again," Colton said under his breath.

"We had words," said Samantha. "I told her in no uncertain terms to leave me alone."

Colton's lips lifted into a partial smile. If only he'd been privy to that conversation. A purple-haired, boot-stomping, name-calling image came to mind, and his smile widened.

Kajsa spied them as she jogged toward the barn.

"I was just taking a quick break," she said, as though worried she'd get in trouble for not working.

"Quick?" Colton questioned, lifting an eyebrow.

Kajsa bit her lower lip. "I wanted to try out her name to see if she'd come, and when she did, I took her back to the corral."

A clang sounded, and Colton looked up to see the mustang lift the lever on the gate with her nose and push it open.

"Why you little . . ." Colton let his words trail off, not wanting to say out loud the word he was thinking.

"Smartypants?" Samantha filled in the blank, making all of them laugh.

"I think I might need your help to catch her again in a bit, Kajsa," said Colton. "You seem to have a knack with her."

"Just call her Your Majesty, and she'll come," answered Kajsa in a matter-of-fact way, as though certain the horse would come when called.

Colton wasn't nearly as certain. He slipped from Nutmeg's back and helped Samantha down as well. "Your Majesty, huh?" he said. The name didn't exactly roll off the tongue. "How did you come up with that?"

"I was working in the barn and it hit me. Before Adi left, she read me a story about a girl who wanted to be a queen so she pretended she was. She had to be in charge and made all of her friends call her 'Your Majesty.'"

Colton didn't make the connection. He'd expected her to come up with a name like Storm or Mad Hatter. Not Your Majesty. What kind of name was that anyway? His brothers would never let him hear the end of it.

"Don't you get it?" Kajsa said.

"Afraid not."

"Your Majesty is just like the girl in that story," she explained. "She wants to be the center of attention and boss people around. So we need to call her Your Majesty. *Now* do you get it?"

Like fitting the right key to a lock, something clicked in Colton's mind—something he'd been trying to figure out since he'd brought the mustang home. Kajsa could be right. The mustang did seem to crave attention. Maybe she'd been the leader of her herd and was used to commanding a crowd. Maybe that's why she'd charged Samantha—because she'd never really focused on the horse. Colton knew because he'd been a little too focused on her.

"You're telling me that when you called out 'Your Majesty,' the horse came?" said Samantha.

Kajsa scuffed the ground with her booted foot before shrugging her shoulders. "Well, I had a carrot too."

Colton laughed. This day had been one of the more interesting days he'd had in a long time, and it wasn't even lunchtime yet.

As Kajsa scampered off to finish her chores, Samantha turned to him with a question in her eyes. "You look like you've just had an epiphany that I don't understand. Your Majesty is a mouthful. Are you sure you want to name the horse that?"

"No. But if the shoe fits . . ." Colton grinned. With one hand on her back and the other clutching the reins, he guided her toward the barn with Nutmeg trailing behind. It felt like the most natural thing in the world to be at Samantha's side, and for a moment, he forgot all about his dislike of temporary things.

The following morning, Kajsa was out of Sam's car before it came to a complete stop. She waved to Colton, who was working with Your Majesty in the corral, and jogged toward the barn—no doubt motivated to get her chores done as fast as possible so she could help with the training.

Sam tightened the yellow bandana around her hair Cinderella-style and forced her still-aching body out of the car. The early morning was cheery and sunny with only a hint of crispness, and the air smelled like hay and nature. She stifled a yawn and stretched her back, letting the peaceful scenery invigorate her. Out in the pasture, Mr. McCoy rode a horse through some sort of obstacle course that she assumed was used for training purposes, while Spencer filled a massive watering trough with a hose. Dustin was probably in the barn with Kajsa.

Sam walked to the corral and stopped a few feet away from the fence. Like yesterday, Colton stood in the center while Your Majesty cantered circles around him. He wore a bright yellow t-shirt, and Sam had to stifle the childish impulse to point to her bandana and say, "Hey, we match."

"Good morning, *Your Majesty*," she said to the horse, wondering if it could detect her sarcasm.

The mustang pulled up short and bobbed its head up and down in an antsy, frustrated way, then trotted to the opposite side of the corral, keeping her back toward Sam.

Colton's rich laughter almost made up for the mustang's bad manners. "I think you just got the cold shoulder," he said. "Apparently Maj is a holder of grudges. What exactly did you say to her yesterday anyway?"

Sam ran her hand over the fence rail and shrugged. "'Say' isn't the exactly the verb I'd use. 'Yelled' is a better word. I'm surprised you didn't hear me."

Colton grinned as he disconnected the lead rope from the harness and gave the mustang a pat on its back. Sam noticed that the gate was now kept closed with a chain and lock, and she had to smile at that. *How are you going to get out now, Your Majesty?*

Real mature, Sam. Real mature.

Colton hopped the fence and stood next to Sam a moment later. "Check it out," he said, gesturing from her bandana to his shirt. "We match."

She grinned. "I was just thinking the same thing. You wore that color on purpose, didn't you?"

"I don't think I've ever worn a certain color on purpose. Why would I?"

"To subtlety hint that I should go back to being a blonde. Admit it."

Colton tapped her bandana. "Is that why you're wearing this? To remind yourself that you'd rather be a blonde?"

"I don't need a reminder. I know I'd rather be a blonde. But I'm stuck with this color for five more days, so until then, I'll be wearing straw-colored hats and yellow bandanas."

He fingered some of her curls, and her shoulder tingled where he brushed it with his hand. "Your hair looks more gray than purple today."

Sam sighed. "I know."

He gave her a quick once-over and raised a brow at her cut-off denim shorts, old U of C t-shirt, and sneakers. "You're not exactly dressed for riding lessons."

"Yeah. My body could use one more recovery day, if that's okay. And I have something better in mind for today." Sam lifted the trunk of her car and gestured inside. "Take a look at some of the most powerful and effective cleaning supplies ever made."

"Some?" Colton's eyes widened at the two boxes filled with everything from cleaning rags, baking soda, and glass cleaner to bleach, bug killer, and air freshener. "What do you plan to do with all that stuff?"

Sam pushed her trunk closed. "Clean The Shack, of course. I wasn't kidding about helping out. It'll be my way of paying you back for my lessons. But I do need you to come down there with me and use those strong muscles of yours"—she tapped his upper arm—"to get me in. My shoulders aren't quite up to bashing in doors just yet."

Colton was already shaking his head. "I don't expect you to pay for riding lessons with hard labor."

"Cleaning isn't hard."

"You haven't tried scrubbing that bathtub yet."

Sam didn't understand why he was arguing. Didn't he say only yesterday that he'd love her help? She folded her arms across her chest and cocked her head at him. "I thought cowboys were supposed to be trustworthy. Yesterday, you said I could help and now I can't?"

"I said you could *help*, not do it all for me. I'm not about to 'bash in the door' and leave you to it. But—"

"Of course you are," she said. "You have a wild and temperamental mustang to train and I'm sure a bunch of other ranching stuff to do. I wouldn't have told you I'm here to clean, but I really do need your shoulder to get me inside."

Colton shifted his weight and stared down the lane, looking like he wasn't quite sure if he should accept her offer or not.

"Pretty please?" Sam said. "Otherwise I can't, in good conscience, let you give me any more lessons."

"I thought you weren't a fan of my teaching methods."

"I have faith in you that they'll go a little better next time."

He snickered. "They can't be much worse, can they?"

"Nope. Now about The Shack. Think of the satisfaction I'll get from making it shine."

He let out a breath and scratched the back of his neck, still not looking overly happy about it.

"Oh, and if there are any dead mice lying around, I'm also going to need you to get rid of them," she added.

"I bet you're going to want the water turned on too."

Her eyes widened, and she laughed. "Yes, I'm definitely going to want water. And power, if that's not asking too much."

His lips pulled into a smile. "You drive a hard bargain."

"I drive a yellow Bug too. Want a ride? I promise that Sunshine is very well behaved and won't jump any fences or throw you out."

"I would only expect that from white Bugs named Herbie."

They both got in the car, and she started the engine. As they drove down the lane, Colton said, "Dare I ask if there's a Sunshine, the first?"

"Yes. It was an old, rust-colored Datsun that used to belong to Emma Grantham before she married Kevin. I loved the name so much that I decided to name my car the same thing even though they're nothing alike."

"Except good for nothing," Colton said under his breath.

Sam pulled to a stop in front of the small cabin and leveled him a look. "I'm sorry. Did you just say my car was good for nothing?"

"No, of course not." He let himself out of the car, and Sam had to jog to catch up to him.

"You did too," she accused.

He shouldered open the door then leaned against the door frame. "I would never say that about a Volkswagen Beetle. I mean, think of all the worthwhile things that car can do. Like look pretty . . . ish on the road or brighten up the road or . . . um . . ."

"Get great gas mileage, turn corners on a dime, be reliable, safe, the perfect size, lovely interior, and just plain fun to drive? That's what you were going to add, right?"

"Right." His lips curved into a smile as he left to carry in her boxes.

While Sam unpacked and figured out where to start, Colton did away with all the dead mice and turned on the water. The power was already on. After making sure the faucets worked and there were no major leaks, he left Sam to do her thing.

From the front window, she watched him walk away. Colton had a casual way about him that made her wonder if he'd ever lost it at a horse. She doubted it. From what Kajsa had said, his workload was heavy, and yet he never seemed stressed. He also made time for Kajsa, a wild mustang, and now Sam.

He disappeared around the corner, and Sam rummaged through the boxes until she found a small speaker. She stuck it in the outlet, plugged her phone into it, and let Fall Out Boy breathe some energy into the tired and dry, creaky space. Then she tugged on some latex gloves and got to work.

Sam bleached the tub, sink, toilet, and grout in the bathroom. She washed windows, stripped the bed, and put the linens in a garbage bag for Colton to either wash or toss out. Inside a small closet, she found an old broom and swept the uneven floor as best she could, wishing she'd thought to bring a vacuum instead. Then she scrubbed the floor and baseboards, wiped down walls, and removed all the cobwebs with a feather duster that would be put to rest outside with the dead mice. So gross.

"Secrets" by OneRepublic came on, and Sam belted out the lyrics while peeling the cover off one of the couch cushions. Something scurried over her feet, and she squealed and leapt onto the arm of the couch, seeing a very-much-alive mouse run across the room and disappear under a TV cabinet in the corner.

With all the traps still scattered around, how was it still alive? The broom leaned against the wall not far away, so she grabbed it, ready to smack the rodent if it showed its fuzzy body again.

The front door burst open with a loud bang, and Sam shrieked again, wielding the wooden broom like a weapon as "Secrets" continued to play on in the background.

Colton eyed her from under the rim of his cowboy hat, not saying anything. He didn't really have to say anything. His what-on-earth-are-you-doing expression said it all.

Sam pointed the broom toward the far corner of the room and squeaked, "Mouse." Not only did she sound like the rodent, but with her purple hair frizzing from underneath the bandana, she probably looked a lot like one too.

Sam really needed to forget the bucket list and dye her hair back to blonde.

Colton approached her the way he might approach a scared or rabid animal and pried the broom from her fingers. Then he strode to the corner, jiggled the TV stand, and whacked the mouse when it came running out. He scooped it up with a dustpan and walked back out, leaving Sam standing on the arm of the couch.

She hopped down and quickly smoothed her hair and retied the bandana. Then she grabbed another couch cushion and was in the process of peeling off the cover when Colton returned.

"Oh, hey," she said, acting as though nothing out of the ordinary had just happened. "Long time, no see."

His lips twitched at the corners. "I came to invite you to a late lunch. Unless you'd rather I fry up that mouse for you instead."

Sickened at the thought, Sam shook her head. "I'll take lunch with your family, thanks."

He walked around the small space, examining all of her hard work. When he finished, he took the cushion from her hands, set it down, and pulled her into a warm and snuggly bear hug that felt better than a soft throw and a mug of rich hot chocolate on a blizzardy day.

"I'm sorry about the mouse," he said quietly in her ear.

Wow, this man knew how to hug. Sam could stay right here forever. "Thanks for getting rid of it."

He pulled back and looked into her eyes. "The house looks incredible. Thank you."

"You're welcome." She liked the way his hand caught hers; the way it felt strong and callused and really, really good.

"Let's go get some grub."

"Let me clean up first, and I'll meet you over there."

Colton nodded toward the front of the house. "I brought the four-wheeler, so I could give you a ride. I'll be on the front porch when you're ready."

He disappeared out the front door, and Sam's heart felt like dozens of tiny butterflies fluttered inside. Every time he glanced her way, touched her, spoke to her, teased her, or laughed, one more butterfly was added to the mix. There was something about Colton McCoy that made her heart want to fly.

Eight

SAM SMILED AT her computer monitor, clicked Print, then arched her back and stretched her arms high overhead. Moments later, the printer spit out a black and white graphic of a small cabin surrounded by scattered trees. Below it, the bolded words "THE SHACK" were spelled out using a western font that Sam had spent hours tweaking. A simple border completed the rest of the design.

Sam smiled, knowing she'd finally gotten it right. She'd spent a week of late-night hours looking for the perfect font, drawing the cabin into illustrator, and adding some trees. The simple lines were rough and imperfect, like it had been rendered using quick swipes of a magnetic doodle pad, but that was the effect Sam had wanted. On the McCoy ranch, there were no clean, straight lines. Everything was just a little rough, muddied, and disorganized. Real.

A few of the carpeted stairs squeaked as she trotted down them. She found her mom and Emma on the back patio, sipping freshly squeezed lemonade and chatting while the twins crawled around on the grass, Maxwell in little khaki shorts and a blue t-shirt and Georgia in a happy, floral sundress. Sam's heart tugged at the thought of leaving in a few months.

She set the recently printed paper on the patio table before capturing Maxwell around the waist and hefting him up to give him a raspberry on his exposed, chubby tummy. All of his shirts fit a little too tight and rode up every time he moved. Maxwell giggled, and Georgia wrapped her tiny arms around Sam's calves.

"Feeling neglected, are we?" Sam dropped down on the grass, let Maxwell escape, and pulled Georgia on her lap. The sweet baby gave Sam's face a hard pat before curling some of her fingers over Sam's lower lip.

"Ow," said Sam, prying them loose. Then she gave Georgia a raspberry on her neck, making her giggle as well.

"I found Georgia trying to suck the lid off a purple marker the other day," said Emma. "I think she was planning to color her hair with it."

Sam set Georgia back down and rose, brushing blades of grass off her denim skirt. "You guys need to lay off the purple jokes. My hair hasn't been that color for days and will never be again."

"Hallelujah," said her mom, holding up Sam's printout of The Shack graphic. "What's this?"

"It's for Colton." Sam took a seat next to her mother. "To say thanks for the riding lessons. I'm going to have it engraved into a Bamboo plaque. What do you think?"

"I think it looks awesome." Her mother handed the picture to Emma. "But haven't you been helping him fix up the place to say thanks for the lessons?"

Sam shrugged. "This is a bonus. I think it'll look great next to his front door."

Emma examined the picture. "This does look amazing. Did you draw the landscape yourself?"

"It's not as good as you could have done," said Sam. Emma was an amazing artist who could pick up a pencil or paintbrush and bring anything to life. Sam, on the other hand, used her mouse and computer. There was a definite art to graphic design, but she would always consider herself more of a cheat and Emma the real thing.

"I disagree. It's beautiful. I love the simplicity of it." Emma handed it back. "I hear you've been spending a lot of time over at the ranch. And what's this about getting chased by a wild horse and nearly killing yourself?"

Sam laughed. "Don't worry. Maj doesn't chase me anymore. She just ignores me."

"Unlike his trainer," said her mother with a sly look.

"Oh please, Mom."

"I've met Colton a few times," said Emma. "He's very nice."

"He is." Sam mentally added funny and clever and gives the best hugs ever—though she wasn't about to say that out loud. Her mother and Emma would pick that up and run a marathon with it.

Not that her mother needed any encouragement. "Oh she thinks he's a little more than nice," said her mom. "Reading between the lines, I'd say she also thinks he's handsome, great with horses and kids, and hilarious. Isn't that right, sweetie?"

Sam chose to plead the fifth, sipping her lemonade instead.

Emma glanced at her babies. "Sounds like a fun summer diversion to me."

"Exactly." Sam shot her mother a pointed look. "He's a *diversion*—not someone who is going to keep me from going to New York." Normally, Sam talked to her mother about pretty much everything, but when it came to Colton, she treaded more lightly. The last thing she wanted was for her mother to get her hopes up that something—or *someone*— could keep Sam in Colorado. New York was the next step in her life—not the McCoy ranch.

Her mother shrugged. "You can't blame a mother for trying."

"Do you really want me to settle down already?" Sam asked. "I'm only twenty-three."

"No. I just don't want you to move to the other side of the country where the crime rate is over three times as high, there are more people than square feet, and studio apartments in a decent section of town cost the same as a big, beautiful home here. How are you going to afford to have any fun with such high rent?" Sam's mother refused to let her get a more affordable apartment in a not-so-decent section of town.

"You know me. I'll make do. Maybe I'll find a room-mate."

"And where would she sleep?" said her mom. "On the floor? Or will you invest in bunk beds?"

"Maybe *he'll* sleep in my bed with me," Sam quipped.

Her mother's eyes narrowed. "Not funny, daughter. Not funny."

Emma laughed. "Sam will be just fine. She's going to prove her worth and be offered a raise in no time."

"It's nice to know somebody has a little faith in me," said Sam.

"I'm your mother. It's my job to worry."

"Just like it's my job to cause you to worry." Sam took a sip of her lemonade, ready to steer the conversation away from anything involving New York or the McCoy ranch or a certain cowboy who was on his way to becoming more than a distraction, though she'd never admit that to her mother. "Speaking of causing you worry, do you happen to know of any reputable pilots around who wouldn't mind letting me jump out of a plane at three or four thousand feet?"

"What?" squeaked her mother.

"Skydiving," said Sam. "It's on my bucket list."

The fence creaked under Sam's weight as she swung her

legs over the top rail and sat down, hooking her boots around a lower rail to keep her balance. The sun hid behind fluffy cumulus clouds that offered some pleasant shade to the ranch. With no breezes to stir the air, it would be a warm day. Colton glanced up from tightening the saddle around Your Majesty's stomach while Kajsa stroked the horse's jaw.

"Hey there, Cowgirl," Colton said to Sam with a smile that made her heart flutter. "When I saw you drop off Kajsa earlier and leave, I figured you had other things going on today."

"I needed to grab something at a store that didn't open until ten. So I ran a few errands, waited for the store to open, and now I'm back. Lucky you." Sam had planned to do other things today, like sculpt some ice or find the perfect mascara, but after picking up a prescription for her father, her thoughts veered in Colton's direction, and she found herself steering her car this way. He'd become a bit of an addiction, and she couldn't find the willpower to stay away. Crossing items off her bucket list didn't sound nearly as fun as riding with Colton or chatting with Colton or fixing up the cabin with Colton or admiring his nice lines as he worked with Your Majesty. Besides, who knew how things would change after today.

In only a few hours, Cassie and Adi would be boarding a flight home, and Sam felt torn. Only fourteen days ago, Sam had yearned for the day when Adi returned so the summer could get back to normal. But now everything would change, and Sam wasn't sure she'd have a reason to drop by the ranch anymore. It wasn't like she could keep asking Colton to give her riding lessons indefinitely.

"I wish I'd known you were coming back," said Colton. "I wouldn't have saddled Maj just yet. We could have gone riding first."

"No worries," said Sam. "I'd rather watch you ride."

"Will you be staying for lunch today, Sam?" Mrs. McCoy's voice came from behind.

Sam swiveled around to find her standing on the front porch. "Hi, Mrs. McCoy. I'd love to stay for lunch, but only if you'll let me help."

"I can always use an extra pair of hands," she answered. "In an hour, come on in, and I'll put you to work."

"Will do."

"Hey, Colt," she called to her son. "Have you seen Spence and Dusty anywhere?"

"Last I saw, they were mucking out the stalls in the boarding stable. I'm assuming they're now helping Dad work with Phoenix. We promised we'd have him ready to go by this weekend."

She nodded. "Just making sure they are up to some good."

"They're never up to any good. You know them."

"Just like their older brother." She gestured toward the mustang. "I take it you're planning to ride her today?"

"Ride. Get bucked off. Repeat. Should be a fun morning."

His mother smiled. "Your definition of fun is very different from mine. Don't forget to come in for some lunch."

Colton's gaze returned to Sam, and he winked. "Wild horses couldn't keep me away."

Sam smiled. Whenever he flirted with her, it melted her insides and turned them into something sweet and yummy, like strawberry jam.

Your Majesty moved forward between Sam and Colton, blocking them from each other's sight. Colton laughed and said, "All right, Maj, you've made your point. I'll pay attention to you now."

From her perch on the fence, Sam studied the mustang. When Kajsa had first psychoanalyzed the animal, Sam had considered it cute—a child's imagined reasoning of an animal's strange behavior. But now the observations fit so well. It was bizarre. Maj was bizarre. She was like a human trapped in a horse's body.

"You finally going to ride that beast?" Dustin hopped on the fence next to Sam, and Spencer followed suit. "Hey, Sam."

"Hey," she answered.

"Don't you two have somewhere you need to be?" said Colton. "Where's Dad?"

"He took Phoenix for a longer ride in the mountains, so we've got some time."

Colton looked like he was about to tell them what they could do with that time when Kajsa piped up, "Let them stay. Maj likes it when everyone is watching."

Colton nodded as though considering it. "Okay. But I want you out of the corral before I mount up."

Her lips formed a pout. "But why? Maj would never hurt me."

"I'd rather be safe than sorry."

"Fine." The soft dirt took all the stomp out of Kajsa's boots, and as she joined the others on the fence, Sam hid a smile. Kajsa was developing a strong personality of her own. No wonder she and Maj got along so well.

The horse had an audience of four people when Colton finally mounted her. She danced sideways as she adjusted to the weight of a rider, but Colton leaned forward and patted her neck, saying something too low for anyone else to hear. She calmed down after that, and although she didn't obey all of Colton's commands—or even most of them—she didn't buck him off either. Colton stayed in the saddle—never raising his voice, only talking and exercising the trait Sam had come to admire most about him: patience.

Did anything get to that man? Day after day, he'd spent hours with that horse, standing in that same corral, taking what had felt like extreme baby steps to Sam. But now, fourteen days into the 100-day competition, he was riding a wild mustang. Sam had seen a lot of beautiful things in her short life, but the scene unfolding before her now touched the artist inside her. The mustang's glistening black coat and powerful, sleek lines. Colton's poise and grace; his charm and patience. The backdrop of dry grass speckled with trees, with a large mountain looming in glorious splendor beyond.

This, right here, was the truest sort of beauty that existed—a moment that couldn't fully be captured by any sort of medium. It had to be breathed, smelled, tasted, felt.

"This is boring," said Dustin, swinging down. "I came for a rodeo and all we got was a dance. C'mon, Spence, let's get those last few stalls cleaned up before Dad comes back."

Sam watched them go, but when the horse gave a loud whinny, she turned back to find the mustang rearing with Colton barely hanging on. The horse came down, kicked up her hind end, and Colton landed on the ground with a thud. Kajsa jumped into the corral and grabbed the reins to calm the horse, and Sam scurried to Colton's side.

"Are you okay?" she asked.

"Just when I start to get a little confident about Maj, she pulls a stunt like that."

"It hurt her feelings when Spencer and Dustin left," explained Kajsa in a matter-of-fact way.

Colton accepted Sam's hand and hefted himself up, brushing as much dirt from his clothes as he could. "Well, she won't always have an audience, Kajsa. How do you propose we teach her to get over her pride?"

Kajsa pursed her lips and finally shook her head. "I don't know. But I'll give it some thought."

Whether or not Colton agreed with Kajsa's assessment of the horse, Sam loved that he made the young girl feel like she was taking part in this training process, that she had thoughts worth voicing, and a voice worth hearing. He'd make a wonderful father one day.

For someone else's kids, Sam forced the thought, even though she felt a stab of envy at the idea of Colton with another woman. What was she thinking? They weren't even dating, and even if they were, Sam would be leaving in a few months for a completely different life in New York. A life that included subways, hustle and bustle, high-rises, pollution, and cityscapes. A life where the only horses she saw would be the ones the policemen rode. A life completely different than this one.

When Sam had first been offered the job, New York had been a bright, gleaming enticement. But now, only two weeks into her summer vacation, it had lost some of its glitter and shine. How would it look in two more weeks? Sam didn't want to go there or even think about going there. Perhaps spending so much time at the McCoy ranch wasn't such a good idea anymore. Maybe it was a good thing Cassie and Adi were coming home today.

A very good thing, she tried to convince herself.

Sam glanced at her watch and took a few steps away from Colton, hooking her thumb over her shoulder. "I should go help your mom with lunch."

The horse whinnied again, and Colton rolled his eyes. "And I should get back on that horse."

"Be careful."

"Always."

In the kitchen, Sam cut up fruit and listened as Mrs. McCoy talked about the McCoy family's summer traditions, including the Fourth of July festivities, the Colorado Springs demolition derby, and the family rodeo.

"What does your family do for the Fourth?" Mrs. McCoy asked.

Sam thought back to past summers. "Kevin always grills something amazing, Emma makes the best homemade ice cream and Texas sheet cake you've ever tasted, my mom whips up her should-be-world-famous-but-isn't-yet potato salad, Dad goes shopping for fireworks in Wyoming, and Noah builds some sort of structure to make the semi-illegal fireworks safe."

"And Cassie?"

"I'm not sure. I spent last summer in North Carolina completing an internship so I wasn't around for that one. Did she and Noah come here?"

"Only for a few hours in the afternoon. But I was thinking that we could do something together this year. Do you think Kevin, Emma, and your parents would be interested in joining us? Though I'm not sure about the semi-illegal fireworks," she added hesitantly. "We live too close to the mountains. But maybe we could do sparklers or something?"

Sam hesitated. Mrs. McCoy had just offered her something she'd been wanting—a reason to come back. But now that it was on the table, did she really want to pick it up? Besides fulfilling one thing on her bucket list, all Sam had really accomplished over the past two weeks was add to the list of people she'd miss when she moved.

"I'll check with everyone and let you know," she finally said.

"Sounds great."

Mr. McCoy came in first, followed by Spencer and Dustin. Lunch was typically served buffet-style on the ranch so that people could come and go whenever they got hungry. Colton and Kajsa showed up last, just as Mr. McCoy and the boys were finishing up.

"How did the riding go?" Sam asked Colton, noting his clothes were dusted with more dirt than before.

"Let's just say that horse belongs in a circus. Not even Kajsa can think of a solution for this one." Colton ruffled her hair, making Kajsa dodge away from his touch. Crazy girl.

While she waited for Kajsa to eat, Sam rinsed what dishes were left in the sink and wiped down counters. As soon as the last bite of sandwich disappeared in Kajsa's mouth, Sam said, "We'd better get going, Kaj."

"Can't we stay a little longer?" she begged.

"I wish we could. But we've got balloons to fill, a banner to paint, and desserts to make." Sam glanced at Mrs. McCoy and explained, "Cassie and Adi are coming home tonight."

"Well, that's happy news." She paused. "Does that mean we won't be seeing you around here as much anymore, Sam?"

"Um . . ." Sam glanced at Colton, who was watching her with interest, as though he might actually care about the answer. "I'm not exactly sure. I mean, I hope I'll be back, but I probably won't be the one driving Kajsa any longer."

Would Colton even care if she didn't drop by anymore? Would he miss her the way she'd miss him? After all of his flirting, he had to care, at least a little. Why wasn't he saying anything?

"We'll miss seeing you as often." Mrs. McCoy filled the awkward silence. "Don't forget to ask your family about the Fourth."

"I won't." The room had suddenly gone from comfortable to stifling, and Sam needed some fresh air. "Thanks again for everything. Kajsa, I'll be waiting outside."

Still no comment from Colton.

On her way out, Sam snagged a carrot off the counter for Nutmeg. She started past the corral where Your Majesty danced, looking restless and confined. Colton hadn't released her to the pasture, so he probably planned to work with her more after lunch.

Sam glanced down at the carrot she held and hesitated. Then she strode toward the corral and stopped on the other side of the fence from Your Majesty. "Tell you what," she said. "I'll give you this carrot if you'll stop throwing Colton."

The horse settled down and scuffed the dirt with one of its hooves. Feeling a bit foolish, Sam held out the carrot. "Well? Do we have a deal?"

Without even sniffing the carrot, Maj turned and pranced away—the kind of prance that belonged in a Disney movie where horses fought humans with frying pans.

"You really need to get over yourself," Sam muttered.

A laugh sounded behind her, and Sam turned to find

Dustin wearing his too-big grin. He rested his elbows on the fence beside her and shook his head. "You know what they say about horses."

"What?"

He took the carrot from her hand and whistled. Moments later, the crazy horse came strutting back and ate that carrot right out of his hand.

Unbelievable.

Dustin's grin widened, and he cocked his head at her. "Horses have a sixth sense about people. If they don't like ya, there's usually a reason."

With a wink and a chuckle, he walked away.

Sam frowned at him then frowned at the horse. She knew Dustin had only been teasing, but for a brief moment, she had a crazy thought.

Is there a reason the horse doesn't like me? Is something wrong with me?

Feeling tried and tested—and lacking—Sam slogged toward her happy, yellow Bug, needing its love more than ever.

Nine

"I BET YOU blink before I do." Sam stared at the clock on her nightstand, challenging it to a staring contest. She rolled onto her stomach and lifted her head from the pillow, forcing her non-sleepy eyes to stay open. The glowing red numbers stared back, taking up the challenge. Several seconds ticked by before the numbers blinked, changing from twelve-forty-seven to twelve-forty-eight.

Triumphant, Sam pointed at the clock. "Told you."

She flopped to her back and focused on the ceiling, blowing a strand of hair out of her eyes. After the ranch in the morning and the welcome home party that evening, it had been a long, busy day. Why wasn't she tired? Why couldn't she fall into the deep and dreamy sleep that usually overtook her by now? Why didn't her pillow-top mattress feel soft and cozy like it usually did?

Sam shifted positions, trying to find a sweet spot. Any sweet spot. When it didn't come, she glared at the clock that now glowed twelve-forty-nine. This was going to be a long night.

Throwing her covers back, Sam padded from her room and down the stairs, trying to avoid the squeaks. She missed the last one, and a loud creak filled the darkness, sounding more than a little creepy.

"Can't sleep either?" The deep voice made Sam jump, and she placed her hand over her heart, squinting at the dark shadow sitting in the armchair next to the fireplace.

"Thanks a lot, Dad," she whispered. "The last thing I need right now is a surge of adrenalin. What are you doing down here?"

"Eating leftover cookies." His hand lifted, holding what looked like a plate. "Want one?"

Sam stole a cookie before plopping down on the sofa across from him and curling her legs beside her. She bit into it, savoring the sweet taste of one of her mother's homemade chocolate chip cookies.

"Aren't you supposed to be on a diet?" she asked her father.

"Supposed to be."

Several months ago, he'd gone in for his yearly physical. When the blood results came back, reflecting a too-high cholesterol number, Sam's mother had immediately instigated a new, healthier eating regimen. But on a night like tonight, when her mother had baked a bunch of cookies for Cassie and Adi's welcome home party, they were left with the inevitable leftovers that her mother couldn't pawn off on anyone else.

"I thought she was going to hide these," Sam mused, taking another bite.

"Your mother can't hide anything from me," said the dark shadow. "I know all her secrets."

"She's going to notice when they're all gone. Or are you planning to replace them with a forged duplicate?"

"I was planning on pointing the finger at you—our beautiful, slender daughter with healthy cholesterol and blood pressure."

"Flattery will get you everywhere. Want some milk?"

"Love some."

Sam stumbled her way to the kitchen and stubbed her toe on a barstool before filling two glasses of milk. She made it back unscathed and handed one to her father. He took a few guzzles and sighed. "Ah, that hit the spot. Thanks, sweetie."

"Anything for you. Just promise you'll hide the evidence."

"I'll be sure to remove all my prints and DNA from the glass before I put it in the dishwasher."

"And I'll leave mine on the counter for Mom to find. She'll never know the truth."

"You are a good daughter."

Sam smiled—at least until her thoughts veered in the direction of the ranch and she remembered a certain horse that might disagree. It would be one thing if Your Majesty believed in equality and treated everyone badly, but the horse had made her preferences obvious. Kajsa was top of her list, with Colton taking a close second, and the rest of the family not far behind. Sam, on the other hand, was the blacked-out name on the very bottom. And it bugged.

"*Am* I good, Dad? I mean, really?" She felt a vulnerability she hadn't felt since—well, ever.

"Why would you ask that? Of course you are."

"Because there's a wild mustang at the McCoy ranch that likes everyone but me."

"I'm sure that's not true."

"I'm not exaggerating. I promise."

Her father took another swig of his milk then set it on the table next to him. "If the horse doesn't like you, it's because she doesn't know you. You, my daughter, are a very likable person."

Sam bit down on her lower lip as she mulled over his words. "I am a likeable person," she said finally.

"You are."

"And if I really wanted to, which I'm not sure I do, I could win over that horse."

"Easy as me finding your mother's hiding places."

Sam wasn't so sure about that, but it was sounding more and more like a challenge, and Sam never backed down from a challenge.

It gives you a reason to go back tomorrow, came a tempting thought.

But you don't want to go back, remember? inserted the voice of reason.

But I do want to go back, thought Sam. *I just don't want to want to go back.*

The lights suddenly flicked on, making Sam gasp and spill a little of her milk on her chest. She twisted around and squinted through the too-bright lights at her mother, who stood at the foot of the stairs, taking in the scene with narrowed eyes.

Busted. Sam slowly turned back to her father, who was pointing a finger at her while his remaining fingers clutched a half-eaten cookie. Next to his elbow sat an empty glass of milk.

Sam rolled her eyes. "You've been caught red-handed, Dad. Maybe if you fess up she'll go easier on you."

"Have you met your mother?" he replied. "It's going to be cabbage, spinach, and broccoli for the next week. I hate broccoli."

"Don't forget Brussels sprouts," said her mother, directing the words at Sam.

Sam frowned. How was that fair? She despised Brussels sprouts. As in, would rather eat seaweed than Brussels sprouts. They tasted like nasty, slimy worms. She twisted around. "Why am I being punished when I'm not on a special diet?"

"It's called guilt by association."

That settled it. Come Monday, Sam would go back to

the McCoy ranch, win over that horse, and hope sweet Mrs. McCoy would invite her to stay for dinner.

Colton hefted the last box from his truck and carried it inside The Shack, dropping it down on the couch. He had to hand it to Samantha. When she offered to help, she really helped. The place practically gleamed it was so clean. The windows had all been washed and scrubbed, the cobwebs eradicated, the warped table sanded and re-lacquered, and a new-to-him taupe shag rug beckoned from under the couch and armchair.

Once it had all come together, Sam had clapped her hands and said, "I told you it would be charming. I love it!"

Colton had to agree. All of Sam's little touches—the vase of fresh flowers on the table, the throw draped over the arm chair that she'd found in the closet, and the family picture she'd gotten from his mother—made the space feel warmer and softer, like her. And if Sam approved, maybe she'd want to come over and hang out sometime. Maybe even a lot of times.

That was before she'd said her goodbyes yesterday.

Colton had known it was coming. She was filling in until Cassie returned from her trip and that was it. But everything had been going so well, and she seemed like she was having a good time. Colton had hoped she'd decide to keep driving Kajsa, or better yet, come on her own with no other reason than to hang out. He wasn't ready to let her out of his life just yet.

Ready or not, though, she was gone, and like it or not, he had to get used to that. Sam wasn't a staying type of girl, anyway. She had too many ambitions. Too many goals. The ranch and Colton had only been a fun little diversion to help pass the time.

He really hated the way his stomach tightened when he thought of never seeing that yellow Bug come up the lane, stirring up a cloud of dust behind it.

Maybe he should have asked her out. Maybe he should have tried to convince her that flings were overrated and that cowboys were underrated.

Footsteps sounded behind him, squeaking the floorboards on the front porch. Colton turned around to find his mother standing there, holding a tinfoil-covered plate of something.

"You left without eating," she said, a little out of breath.

"I ate a bowl of cereal and a piece of toast."

"That's not a breakfast." She shoved the plate into his hands. "This is a breakfast."

Colton could feel that the food was still warm, and it smelled wonderful. "Thanks, Mom. But I'm moving out of the house to become more independent, and that means making my own breakfast."

"Or pouring it from a cardboard box?" She made a face, and he smiled.

"Or pouring it from a cardboard box."

She let out a sigh that sounded like I-may-not-like-it-but-its-your-life-to-live then looked around, walking farther into the room. "Wow, you really cleaned this place up."

"It was mostly Samantha's doing."

His mother toed the rug. "Is this new?"

"Samantha brought it over. One of her mom's client's was moving and didn't want it anymore, so Samantha showed up with it a few days ago, rolled up and sticking out the back of her trunk." Colton smiled at the memory. Maybe the little yellow Bug was good for something after all.

"It looks nice."

"I think so."

She cocked her head to the side and eyed her son. "You two seem to get along so great that I thought you might . . ." her voice drifted off, and she waved her hand. "Well, never mind. I guess I thought wrong."

"I like her, but I really don't think she'd be interested in a guy like me long-term."

"Why would you say that?"

Colton set the plate on the counter and opened and closed a few drawers before he found the cheap silverware he'd picked up at the store last week. He pulled out a fork and palmed the counter. "She's too spontaneous and adventurous for ranching life. Coming here . . . well, it was something new and exciting to experience. But now that she's experienced it, she'll move on to something else that's new and exciting. Trust me."

His mother walked forward, placing her hands on the side of his face. "I'm only going to say this once, because, like you moving to The Shack, I know you need to live your own life your own way. But I can't let a comment like that slide with no response. You are handsome, talented, hardworking, and—most importantly—a good man. A girl would have to be blind not to see that. But if you find a girl you're interested in and don't make your interest clear, she might walk out of your life for the same reasons you're letting her walk out."

His mother gave his cheek a pat, and her expression softened. "I like Sam. A lot. And I'm pretty sure that she likes you. No girl would help you do all this"—she gestured around her—"if she didn't. But if you're not willing to do anything about that then . . . perhaps it's a good thing she won't be coming around much anymore."

She blew a kiss to her son and walked out the door, leaving him with some food for thought as well as food for his stomach. For the first time since meeting Samantha and reading her crazy bucket list, Colton considered doing more than offering her riding lessons, accepting her help with The Shack, and saying nothing when she said goodbye. His fork tapped against the counter as he considered what exactly "more" would entail.

Out the large front window, a yellow Bug puttered down the lane, passing by The Shack on its way to the ranch. Kajsa sat in the passenger seat with her hand flying through the air, and adjacent to her was a perky profile wearing a tarnished-straw cowboy hat.

Colton tossed the fork in the sink and slid the breakfast plate into the microwave before walking into the slightly overcast June morning. There was a good possibility that Sam was only here because Cassie had too much going on and needed her to drive one last time, but Colton still considered it a second chance. This time, when she said goodbye, he wouldn't sit by and do nothing.

Ten

COLTON STRODE TOWARD the main house, feeling lightness in his feet and anxiousness in his chest. The last time he'd been this excited about a girl, they'd dated for a month before she informed him that she was looking for a man with a little more sophistication. Initially, her rejection had wounded him until he realized she was right. She'd loved her high heels, her flouncy skirts, and her perfect, pale complexion. She hadn't loved the ranch—or Colton, as it turned out.

Samantha, on the other hand, had embraced everything about his life—bumps, bruises, dead mice, wild horses, and all. If Colton didn't at least try to see what could happen, he'd always wonder.

As he approached the house, Samantha stood next to the corral, waving a long carrot with bushy green stems at Maj. A few roots dangled from the end as though she'd just plucked the vegetable from the ground. Maj stood on the opposite side of the corral, making no move to accept her offering. She sniffed and stomped the ground with her front hoof.

Samantha raised her voice. "I'll have you know, this is no ordinary carrot. It's an expensive, home-grown, *organic* carrot that I picked up at the farmer's market this morning for no one else but you. Are you really going to turn your nose up at it? Because I know plenty of other horses who would love it."

Maj turned around, directing her backside toward Samantha.

The carrot dropped to Samantha's side, and she frowned. "Fine. I'll just give this to Nutmeg then." She took a slow step sideways, as though making a show of following through with her threat.

Colton had to bite his lip to keep from laughing and giving himself away. Did she really think reverse psychology would work on a horse?

Sam stopped. "Actually, you know what? I think I'm going to eat the carrot myself instead." She ripped off the roots before taking a small bite and munching it. Then she crawled to the top of the fence, swung her legs over, and took another bite. "Mmm, this is the best carrot I've ever eaten. You sure you don't want any?"

Maj responded by sniffing at a small cluster of weeds near a post and munching on that.

Sam's jaw dropped. "Seriously? You'd rather eat weeds? What are you trying to prove anyway? That you're more stubborn than me? That you'd rather eat garbage than give me the time of day? What is so wrong with me anyway? I am a likeable person. Ask anyone—even my dad. He'll tell you—"

Colton coughed out a laugh—he couldn't help it.

Samantha spun around and nearly lost her seat on the fence as she gaped at him. "How long have you been standing there?"

Colton rested his elbows on the fence next to her, still grinning. "If you're going to use your father as an

92

endorsement, I wouldn't call him dad. It removes all credibility."

Samantha stepped off the fence and handed over the carrot. "I'll give you twenty bucks if she stiffs you, too."

The moment the vegetable exchanged hands, Maj glanced over her shoulder and gradually meandered her way across the corral to where Colton stood.

Instead of feeding the mustang the carrot, Colton took Samantha's hand and placed the carrot on her palm, curling her fingers around it. Still holding her hand, he held out the vegetable. "If you want this carrot," he said to Maj, "you're going to eat it from both of us."

Maj sniffed, bobbed her head a few times, then walked away. Sam immediately pried her hand free and tossed the carrot in the corral. Then she turned her back on the horse and folded her arms in frustration. It was an adorable look on her.

Colton leaned a shoulder against the fence. "Why do you suddenly want her to like you so much?"

"Because she likes everyone else. And if I'm the only one she can't stand, what does that say about me?"

Colton watched her a moment longer before clearing his throat. "I can't speak for the horse, but I like you just fine."

Colton wanted to gag on his own words. *Just fine?* Had he really made it sound like she was an average pair of jeans that he liked *okay*?

"Um . . . wow, you sure know how to make a girl feel better," said Samantha, obviously unimpressed by his pathetic attempt at a compliment.

"I'm sorry. That came out wrong. What I meant to say is that I like you. A lot. In fact, I'm hoping you'll agree to go out with me this weekend."

Her brows drew together. "If you're only asking me because you want to make me feel better, I'd rather you didn't. There's nothing worse than a pity date."

"It's not a pity date."

"You sure?"

"Let me put it this way. If you tried to feed me a carrot, I'd eat it in a heartbeat."

Her eyes widened briefly before a giggle escaped from her mouth. "I can't believe you just said that."

"And I can't believe you haven't said yes yet."

"I, um—"

From across the corral Maj whinnied, as though she realized the attention was no longer on her. Colton waved a hand in a dismissive way, his eyes still focused on Samantha. Not many girls could pull off the cowboy hat the way she could. She'd chosen one with style; one that complemented her green eyes, high cheekbones, and fountain of curls, and yet there was no pretense or show about her—as though she had no idea how gorgeous she looked or how attractive he found her.

He cocked his head to the side, wishing his heart would stop hammering. "So how 'bout it? Is it date or not?"

She hesitated a moment longer before giving him a slight nod. "All right, cowboy. It's a date."

Colton took one step back, then two, trying to keep himself from grinning like an idiot. "I'll pick you up at six-thirty on Friday." Then he turned around and headed toward the barn.

"Wait. Where are we going?"

"That's for me to know and you to find out."

"But how should I dress?"

He turned back and let his eyes take her in a moment longer. A light breeze lifted her hair, the shade from her hat darkened her eyes, and her pink shirt and dark jeans hugged her beautiful curves. "You look perfect exactly as you are."

Her brow wrinkled and she looked down at her clothes. "Please tell me I can wear something besides a hat, boots, and jeans."

Colton lost the battle to the grin. "Wear whatever you'd

like, but keep in mind that you just agreed to go out with a cowboy." He continued toward the barn, pretending not to hear her mutter, "That's not helpful."

He chuckled as he passed through the door and into the muggy barn, mentally patting himself on the back for converting a goodbye into a see-you-soon.

Keep in mind you agreed to go out with a cowboy, Sam thought of Colton's words as she studied her reflection, not happy with the same old boring jeans, the same straw hat, and the same brown boots. Why couldn't she wear her favorite wedge sandals, the knee-length white, eyelet skirt that made her feel flirty and feminine, and the turquoise blouse that brightened her eyes? She could have looked fantastic tonight. Instead, she looked her usual, non-wowing normal.

Years ago, her mother had invented the "At Least" game for times such as these, when a situation called for pessimism and they wanted to turn it around. Sam had used it so much it had become second nature.

At least these jeans have a cute design on the back pockets. At least I can wear my hair down. At least this top is a little dressier than normal—or, as dressy as I can pull off with jeans.

The pessimistic thoughts remained, so she tried again.

At least I'm going out with Colton McCoy.

Her lips lifted into a smile as she donned her tattered straw hat. That's what she needed to remember. Colton.

The doorbell rang, and Sam's gaze flew to her clock. He was ten minutes early. Who came ten minutes early to a date?

She grabbed her purse and keys and trotted downstairs to find not one, but both of her parents at the front door.

Her mother was doing the talking. "I'm Becky, and this is my husband, Justin. You must be Colton. We've heard so much about you."

"Pleasure to meet you both," answered Colton, his gaze locking on Sam as she landed at the bottom of the stairs, slightly out of breath.

"Would you like to come in for a moment?" her mother said.

Sam pushed her way through her parents to find Colton wearing black jeans, a fitted, gray and blue plaid, button-down shirt, and a matching black hat. How did he look so much better than every other day when he was wearing the same cowboy garb? Not fair.

She slipped her arm through his and tugged him toward the door. "We really need to be going, don't we?"

Colton was either clueless or contrary because he wouldn't budge. "Not yet. I would love to come in, if that's okay."

"You really don't have to," said Sam. "They bite."

"So do horses." He winked, pulling her toward the door.

"Finally," her mother said as they passed, lifting her hands to the heavens. "A man who can stand up to Sam. We like you already, Colton."

"That was easy," he whispered in Sam's ear.

"Just remember, you brought this on yourself." She settled on the loveseat next to him, feeling strangely nervous. It had been a long time since she'd had to take part in a pre-date get-to-know-you session with her parents. Roommates were so much less invasive.

"So tell me, Colton," her father began. "Where do you see yourself in five years?"

"Dad!" Samantha protested, glaring at her father. "He's joking," she added to Colton.

"Am I?" her father said.

"Yes," answered her mother. "You are."

Colton actually chuckled. "I don't mind answering the question, sir."

"Really?" Her father looked surprised, maybe even a little impressed. And who could blame him? Sam was pretty impressed herself.

"I guess I see myself doing much the same thing as I did today. Feed and train horses, clean out the tack room, teach a few young people how to ride, and repair some fencing. Our ranch is land-locked and too small for the cattle business, so there aren't many opportunities for growth. One day I hope to take over, just not anytime soon."

"So you plan to stay here in *Colorado*," her mother emphasized, shooting a pointed glance at her daughter.

"Yes, ma'am." Colton looked confused. He was probably thinking, *Isn't that what I just said?*

"Are you planning to take over the ranch because you want to?" asked her father.

"Yes, sir. I love working with my hands and with animals and being outdoors. It's a dream job for me."

More questions came from both of Sam's parents. They asked about the history of the ranch, about Colton's family, and about how the training was going with the wild mustang. Colton answered them all with confidence and wit, always addressing her parents as ma'am and sir. Sam's nerves settled, and she relaxed against the back of the loveseat, wondering what she'd been worried about. Colton was a pro at this, as though he'd done it a million times before.

Sam frowned at that thought.

"Tell me, Colton," her father finally said. "Does Maj really hate Sam as much as she says?"

Colton grinned. "Yes, sir. According to Kajsa, the mustang is very jealous of your daughter."

"Jealous?" asked her mother.

"The horse likes to be the center of attention, and—" Colton looked at Sam in a way that made her heart leap, prance, and canter. "Well, let's just say that when your daughter's around, the horse doesn't get nearly as much attention. Samantha's like the sun—cheery, bright, and warm. Kind of hard to resist that, and Maj knows it."

Sam's heart triple-thumped, and a rich, heavenly sensation spread through her body. Three sentences and Maj not liking her became a compliment instead of a flaw. She could have hugged Colton for that.

"Sam does have a very sunny personality," said her mom. "We used to call her Sunny when she was a toddler."

"Sunny, huh?" Colton chuckled, and Sam rolled her eyes. That was one nickname she wished her mother had kept to herself.

"What sort of things do you do for fun on the ranch?" her father's voice came again.

"Lots of things, but the big event happens at the end of July. Every year, my parents host a small, family-and-friends style rodeo. One neighbor brings over a bronc or two, another some cows for roping, and another some sheep for mutton busting. My brother, Spence, dresses up as a clown, and I play the part of the emcee. Then Cider and Whisper—two of our horses—are used for barrel racing. My dad barbeques hamburgers and hot dogs, and my mom whips up the tastiest fruit salad and mint brownies you've ever eaten."

Her father's expression became very interested. "Did you just say mint brownies?"

"You're more than welcome to join us, sir. You too, ma'am."

"And you're welcome at our house anytime," added her mom.

"Thank you. I appreciate that." Colton stood and replaced his hat, then offered his hand to Sam. "We'd better get going or we'll be late. It was a pleasure to meet you both."

"Have fun tonight," said her mother.

After a moment of hesitation, Sam clasped his hand. It felt warm and rough and wonderful, just like she knew it would. On their way out, she envisioned her mother doing a happy dance the moment they closed the door. Because if anyone could convince her daughter that going to New York was a bad idea, it was Colton McCoy.

Eleven

"YOU BROUGHT ME to a rodeo?" asked Sam as they passed street vendors selling everything from hot dogs and slushies to cowboy boot refrigerator magnets. She'd never seen so many cowboy hats, Wranglers, or big belt buckles.

"You did say you wanted to ride a bull," Colton said.

For a second, fear seized Sam's heart, until she remembered, "You have to be a professional to ride in a rodeo. Don't you?" *Please say yes.*

"This is just an amateur rodeo. Anyone can sign up."

Anyone? As in *Sam*—a twenty-three-year-old horseback-riding novice? Sam grabbed Colton's arm and stepped in front of him, stopping their progress toward the arena. "Sign up? That's something I should have done before now, isn't it?"

"Yep." He clasped her elbow and steered her toward the arena. "Good thing I took the liberty of doing it for you. You'll be riding a bull named Kabookie."

Kabookie? What sort of name was that? It sounded like a combination of crazy and mean, like a nickname for a serial killer. Sam glanced down at her clothes. Had she really worn this cute, red top to get tossed and trampled by an animal named Kabookie?

"Um . . . about that list," said Sam. "I was actually planning to make a few, you know, revisions?"

"I thought it was set in stone."

"Well, it is. But . . ." She bit her lip, wondering how to tell him that she'd dye her hair permanently purple before she'd ever strap her hand to the back of a bull. Yet he'd gone to the trouble of signing her up, asking her out, and bringing her here. Had he even paid an entrance fee for her to ride?

"I thought you said I should move bull riding to the bottom of my list because—how did you put it? Oh, that's right—I might *die* doing it?"

"I was only joking about that," he said with a wave of his hand. "Only about three people die every year from bull riding, so really there's only a point-two percent chance that tonight will be the end of you."

"Did you really just say *only*?" said Sam. How could anyone use the word "only" in any sentence that included the word "die"? If a statistician were to take into account Sam's level of experience—or lack thereof—she was certain that point-two would become ninety-six, with only a four percent chance of sheer dumb luck saving her.

Colton put his arm around her shoulders and pulled her close. "You're not really afraid of a two-thousand pound animal with horns are you?"

Horns! How had Sam forgotten about those? If she didn't get trampled, she was sure to get skewered. Suddenly, her four percent chance of surviving dropped to zero.

What sort of person decided bull riding should be a sport anyway? Probably a descendent of the person who thought the gladiator games would be a hoot. Both of them could have used a good psychologist.

"Do you or don't you want to check bull riding off your bucket list?" Colton had stopped in front of a red, white, and blue inflatable with a large mechanical bull in the center. A gaudy looking sign stood off to the side.

Ride Kabookie
Only $10

Sam looked from the sign to Colton as it all sank in. Kabookie was made of metal and gears, not two thousand pounds of flesh, blood, and muscle. There would be no hand tying, no horns piercing her middle, and no hoofs crushing her ribs and lungs. She would live another day.

Sam sighed in relief, then immediately slapped Colton's arm. "I can't believe you did that to me. What kind of date are you?"

He laughed the deep, reverberating laugh that made a bunch of people stop and take note. He didn't seem to have any idea how good it sounded, how amazing he looked tonight, or how much Sam wanted to throw her arms around him and plant a kiss on those grinning lips.

Colton handed the attendant a ten dollar bill and gestured for Sam to take her ride. She wobbled her way to the middle of the inflatable and crawled on the beast's back.

"What setting would you like it at, ma'am?" asked the man.

"As high as you've got." After freaking out about riding a real bull, Sam wasn't about to let a mechanical version make her look even more wimpy.

"You sure?" Colton said.

"Positive." She nodded toward the attendant. "All the way up."

"You asked for it."

Sam listened to a brief instructional, then held on tight as the bull began moving forward and back, spinning in slow circles. *This is easy*, she thought, her body moving with the machine. She was about to call out, *Hey, is this all you've got?* when the bull began to pick up speed. One jerk, two, and her fingers were ripped from the handholds. She flew through the air and landed in an awkward lump on the not-so-cushy plastic inflatable.

Colton's low chuckle sounded as she picked herself up, retrieved her hat, and adjusted her top. She wobbled her way back to Colton and, without saying anything, took her purse and rifled through it, finding another ten dollar bill. She handed it to the attendant. "It's his turn now, and he also wants the highest setting."

"Oh no, that's okay—" Colton started to argue.

"You're not afraid of a little mechanical bull, are you?" she challenged. After what he'd just put her through, he deserved to get tossed too.

He shook his head and shrugged, then pressed his hat down over his head before walking across the inflatable with a lot more grace and swinging onto the back of the robotic bull. He waved off the man's offer for a tutorial then rode the beast like it was a kiddy ride at the state fair. It didn't matter which way the bull jerked, how fast it "bucked," or which direction it spun, Colton made it look effortless. His arm waved behind him like a pro, his muscled torso kept him in place, and his hat stayed squarely on his head.

Sam wanted to ask for her ten dollars back.

Cheers and clapping broke out around them, and she realized Colton had acquired an audience. He jumped off the bull without appearing dizzy or out of breath and tipped his hat to the crowd. When he rejoined Sam, there was no gloating. Only, "Ready to go watch real bull riding now?"

"You're amazing," Sam blurted, blinking up at him. He reminded her of one of those hidden picture puzzles in a *Highlights* magazine. At first glance, he was the image of a handsome cowboy front and center on the page, but inside that image were a lot of really cool traits just waiting to be found.

A dormant part of Sam's heart seemed to yawn and stretch and flutter its eyes.

Sam frowned and looked away, trying to lull that part of her heart back to sleep. She didn't want it to wake up. Not yet. It wasn't time. "So, um . . . do you really think riding a mechanical bull counts towards my list?"

"You didn't specify a living, breathing bull, did you?"

"No."

"Then it counts."

Colton held out his hand, and she took it tentatively, feeling a vulnerability she'd never experienced with a guy before. His fingers interlaced through hers, bringing more warmth, more depth, and more conflicting emotions. All she could think was that her hand had never fit so well in anyone else's.

They found their seats, and Colton sat snug beside her on the bench. Their shoulders bumped every time they moved, causing an echoing thump in her heart. It was difficult to concentrate on the rodeo with the scents of leather and soap in the air, the touch of his arm against hers, and the sight of the smile he flashed her way.

"You've got to love the diversity of people who gather at rodeos," Colton said, apparently not as affected as her.

Sam forced her gaze to the stands surrounding the arena. There were old people and young people, dressed-up people and dressed-down people, blue-collars, white-collars, and rednecks. Babies hollered, kids squabbled, and adults chatted. It occurred to Sam that the rodeo was a place for anyone and everyone. She liked that. She liked the energy that buzzed through the arena when the emcee's voice sounded through the loudspeakers. And she liked her date. A lot.

Colton was great about explaining each event, along with the judging process. Between events, they talked about life in college and how great it had been to grow up in Colorado Springs. They laughed at the clown and the wild cow-milking fiasco and sipped lemonade slushies during intermission. They gasped when riders were thrown from broncs or charged by bulls and sighed when the rodeo ended without contributing to the three deaths per year.

Dust and the smell of livestock lingered in the air as Colton guided her through the crowds with his palm on the small of her back, and Sam felt like she'd never been on a more perfect date. As they crossed through the parking lot, his hand found hers again.

During the drive home, he asked her about her family, and she asked him about what it was like to grow up in the country and go to school in the city. He pulled to a stop in front of her house, and they continued to talk about trivial things and serious things, funny things and nothing in particular.

It wasn't until Sam's phone vibrated with a text from her mother that she realized how late—or early—it was.

"Oh, wow. It's already one o'clock. I'm so sorry I've kept you up so late."

"Don't be," said Colton. "I'm not."

"You'll probably be singing a different tune when your alarm clock goes off in the morning." She pushed the door open and hopped out. Colton met her outside and wrapped an arm around her shoulders as they sauntered up the walk. On the porch, he pulled her into a tight bear hug, resting his chin on top of her head.

The clean, leathery scent that had teased her all night long filled her nostrils, and his strong, warm body felt like a perfect complement to hers.

What would tomorrow bring? Or the next day? Or the next? If he asked her out again, would she say yes?

"Thanks for giving me an opportunity to ride a bull, and for being so upfront and honest about it." Her palms slid from around his back to his chest, where they lingered. "I have to admit, you had me worried for a minute."

"I had you sweating, you mean."

"I never sweat. That's not ladylike. I only perspire." She tapped his chest with her finger then stepped out of his arms and into early morning air that felt cool and a little bit scratchy. Only a few hours earlier, the air had been perfect. Not too cold, not too hot. Just inviting, invigorating, and welcoming. Now, sans Colton, it had lost its coziness.

The sound of her phone vibrating in her purse filled the silence, reminding Sam that she hadn't texted her mother back. "That's my mom. She's a worrier. I should go."

Colton leaned in, and his lips hovered near hers for a moment before landing softly on her cheek at the side of her mouth. "Goodnight Samantha," he whispered before walking away.

Her cheek pulsed where he'd touched it, and her chest rose and fell as though he'd just left a searing kiss on her lips. She touched the spot tentatively and chided her emotions. It was a peck on the cheek! A peck! Something her grandma or father would have given her. Nothing to get all shaky over.

But it hadn't felt like a simple peck. It had felt like a beginning.

Twelve

SAM HAD BEEN on good dates before. Even great dates. She'd crawled in bed with a smile on her face, thinking back on a particular guy and how fun he'd been or how great he'd kissed. Sometimes, she'd even dreamed about him.

But until now, nobody had ever kept her from sleeping.

Even though she hadn't known Colton long—three weeks was nothing—Sam felt like the strands of her soul had snaked out and connected with someone else's—a solid enough connection that it made her worry about the distance between Colorado and New York and how far that connection could be stretched before it broke.

Years ago, on the night of Sam's sixteenth birthday, her mother had walked into her room and pulled Sam's journal from her bookcase. She'd plopped down at the foot of Sam's bed and handed the journal to her daughter.

"You're moving into an important phase of your life where you'll start thinking about the future and what kind of person you'll want to walk down the aisle toward someday. I want you to date a lot—all different kinds of people—and every time you do, I want you to come home and write down the qualities of that person you liked or didn't like—the qualities that are important to you in a future husband and father. Yes, attraction is important, but I want you to look deeper than that. Harder. Go beyond good hair, handsome faces, and great bodies and into minds and hearts. How does he treat other people? How does he treat you? Is he driven? Does he care about learning, about improving, about working hard and doing his best? Does he care about you and your opinions and how you feel? Does he have faith in God? Is he a good person? Does he see the real you?"

Sam fingered the journal. Her mother was rarely this serious, and Sam wasn't sure how to respond. "Wow, this is kind of a deep conversation for midnight."

Her mother had leaned forward and placed a hand on Sam's knee. "The kind of guy you decide to date and eventually marry will affect the rest of your life. Whatever you do, *don't* make that decision lightly. Take your time. Become the kind of person you'd want to marry and find someone whose strengths will make you better, someone whose weaknesses complement yours. Find someone you can really connect with—physically, emotionally, and intellectually. And then date him a long time to make sure."

Her mother gave her knee a squeeze. "Sam, you're beautiful and spunky and confident. You're going to attract all sorts of guys. Weed out the creeps, date the others, and keep a list. It will change and evolve as you grow and mature, but one day you'll meet someone different—someone special—someone who has the most important qualities you've written down and throws in some extras that you hadn't thought of before. He won't be perfect, and neither will you, but he'll be the sort of man you can count on to stick by your side through all the bumps and lumps of life. Be wise. It's the most important decision you'll ever make."

After her mother had left, Sam propped up her pillows, borrowed a pen from her nightstand, and tapped it against her lower lip as she considered her mother's words. Then she began The List—one that had evolved over the years just like her mother had said it would. She'd crossed out some things, revised others, and added to it.

The only time she hadn't pulled out the journal after a date was tonight.

Through the darkness, Sam could make out the white outlines of her bookcase. Even though she couldn't see the journal, she knew exactly where it was located. It seemed to call out to her, telling her to open it up and take a look.

But Sam didn't need to open it up to see. She had The List memorized.

Good sense of humor. Makes me smile and laugh.

Someone I connect with

~~*Tall, dark, and handsome.*~~ (Meant as a joke in the beginning, then later changed to) *Attractive*

Treats me with respect

Loves kids, especially Adi and Kajsa. And Maxwell and Georgia.

~~*Is not obsessed with Taylor Swift*~~ (She eventually crossed this out because she couldn't imagine meeting another guy with a room plastered in Taylor Swift paraphernalia. He'd only asked Sam out because she sort of looked like the teen icon. Gag.)

Appreciates good art. (After she'd taken Damien to an art exhibit, she'd added,) *Even if I have to explain why it's good.*

Works hard

A great kisser (Added after Milton had given her the goodnight kiss of all goodnight kisses. Who would have thought someone named Milton could have kissed like that?)

Athletic. ~~*Into sports like basketball or running.*~~ *Wants to be healthy and active.* (Revised after dating*

Rex—a lover of yoga and long walks)

Shows kindness to everyone, especially his family. (After Steven came to a summer barbeque and didn't make an effort to get to know anyone, Sam added,) *And mine*

Has to be willing to watch what I want to watch sometimes (Added after Clayton reluctantly agreed to watch The Princess Bride and ended up loving it)

Cares about school and learning

Supports me in my goals (Added after Weston tried to talk her out of accepting what turned out to be a fantastic summer internship)

Loves to have fun. (Then, after she dated the all-about-fun-and-nothing-else Brian, added,) *But also has a serious side*

A great cook (Added after Beckett made her the most amazing fried tacos she'd ever tasted. If only he'd had some of the other qualities on her list.)

Sam knew that if she pulled out that journal and let Colton factor in, her mother's words, spoken so long ago, would be like an ancient prophesy that was finally coming true. *One day you'll meet someone different—someone special—someone who has the most important qualities you've written down and throws in some extras that you hadn't thought of before.* Sam began to think of all the extras.

Rides mechanical bulls with finesse
Tames wild horses
Looks amazing in a cowboy hat and Wranglers.
Has a laugh that stops people in their tracks. In a good way.
Cares about animals
Lives in the cutest little shack ever built
Has the patience of Job

Can win over my parents in a matter of minutes
Someone I can talk to for hours, but it feels like
only minutes

The only problem was that Sam had another list—one that had been imbedded in her mind rather than scribbled on paper. It didn't need adaptations or revisions. It had been the same ever since she decided what she wanted to be when she grew up.

Get accepted to a good graphic design program
Maintain at least a 3.75 GPA
Land a competitive internship
Graduate with honors
Go to work for a premier design firm for at least
two years
Start my own company and make it successful

Unlike The List, this one was numbered. Like stepping stones, each step brought her closer to her ultimate goal. And now she was almost there. Jason Brecken Design was ranked number four of the best graphic design companies in the world. Not just the US, the *world.*

How many people had applied for the coveted junior designer position?

Over three hundred.

How many people had been offered the job?

One.

Sam.

Why? Because her portfolio was fantastic, because she'd worked her tail off, because Vinyasa—the company she'd interned with—had given her a gushing recommendation, and because she'd nailed all four of the interviews.

Come late August, little Samantha Kinsey of Colorado Springs would be part of the team involved in creating identities, designing websites, apps, commercials, and film, along with album covers for artists like Coldplay, Imagine Dragons, and Fun. How could she walk away from that? She couldn't. It was the opportunity of a lifetime—a spectacular, gilded stepping stone along her career path.

Sam grabbed her pillow and pressed it over her face as she realized the direction her thoughts had veered. What was she thinking? It had been one date. One night of her life. That's it. These were crazy thoughts. Premature thoughts. Drama-queen thoughts.

She groaned into her pillow then flipped to her side and glared at her clock. Five o'clock. This was ridiculous. Thank goodness she didn't have to take Kajsa to the ranch in the morning. She'd show up a bleary-eyed mess and find Colton looking as awake and alert as always. He was probably sleeping like a baby right now.

Go to sleep. Go to sleep. GO TO SLEEP, she yelled at her inner thoughts.

Sam conjured up a flock of sheep in her mind and began counting them. But when black cowboy hats appeared on little furry heads, she groaned again.

It was useless. She needed to get her mind on something else, and she needed to do it pronto. Sam tossed her covers aside, grabbed a novel from her bookcase, fished a flashlight from her nightstand, and crept down the stairs. The patio door squeaked when it opened, but the rest of the house remained silent. She dropped into her father's hammock and left one leg dangling over the side. Back and forth she swayed, listening to the peaceful chirping of the early-rising birds. A soft glow melted across the horizon, paving the way for the sun to rise. Her body relaxed, and her eyelids grew heavy. This was exactly what she needed. A change of scenery.

Sam turned her face away from the glow, wishing she'd thought to come out here earlier, before the stars had disappeared. Then maybe she would have been able to check "Sleep under the stars" off her bucket list. Perhaps she still could. The stars were glittering somewhere in the vast universe even if they weren't visible.

Thirteen

"SAM," A GENTLE VOICE cooed, bringing Sam back from a world of elephant-sized chirping birds and miniature sheep wearing Stetsons. Warm hands grasped her shoulders, giving her a little shake. Her eyes drifted open to see her mother staring down at her.

"What are you doing out here?"

Sam stretched and yawned, then snuggled into the hammock once more. "Trying to sleep. Go away."

"How long have you been out here?"

"I don't know. What time is it?"

"Almost noon."

Noon. Oh good. At least she'd gotten a few hours of sleep, though her body still cried out for more.

"Honey, I've been looking everywhere for you. I've texted, called, finally found your phone but not you. Couldn't you have at least left a note, a clue, something?"

"I left the back door unlocked," Sam murmured, grateful for the shade her mother's body provided. The cooler air felt wonderful.

"Honey." Another shake of Sam's shoulders, and her

eyes reopened. "Seriously, why are you out here? You only sleep somewhere else when something's bothering you. And the entire left side of you is red. You need to get out of the sun."

Red? Sam's palms flew to her face, feeling the difference in temperature between her cheeks. Squirming to a sitting position, she inspected her nearly hot pink arms.

"Fabulous," she groaned. Not even her good concealer could cover up a solid sunburn. No wonder most people preferred to sleep under the stars instead of under the sun. The stars were kinder.

Her body rolled from the hammock and she trotted inside, going straight to the half bath next to the kitchen. She groaned again. Her face looked like the flag of Indonesia turned on its side.

Are you kidding me? she thought.

"Why can't my skin just tan?" she grumbled as she glared at her reflection. It would be easy to return to the hammock and let the right side of her body catch up to her left. But having been cursed with pale, tanless skin, her entire face would turn red.

Maybe if she put some ice on it . . .

Sam dashed past her mother to the freezer and grabbed a bag of frozen peas. Pressing them against the left side of her face, she noticed her mother watching her with an expectant *Well? I'm waiting.*

Sam dropped down on a barstool and propped her arm up on the table. "I couldn't sleep, so around five I went out back to read and fell asleep in the hammock. Sorry I didn't leave any clues other than an unlocked back door."

"Is there a reason you couldn't sleep?"

Sam bit her lower lip, wishing she could trust her mother to be impartial. But her mother wasn't impartial. She was pro Sam-folding-in-her-wings and staying put in Colorado. And that made her the last person Sam wanted to talk to about this.

"I think there was a pea under my mattress," she finally said.

"And now there's a bag of peas next to your face."

Sam considered the frozen vegetable. What would happen if she mashed the peas into a gooey mush and applied it to her face as a mask? Maybe she would discover that the tiny vegetables were really an unknown natural remedy that could draw the red out of sunburns. Sam could design an attractive label for it, market it, become a millionaire, and not have to worry about sticking to her career goals any longer.

Problem solved.

Her mother sighed. "Okay, fine. If you don't want to tell me, I won't force it out of you. But I'm always here for you if you need to talk. And I mean that in a figurative way because I have to run to meet a client right now. Are you sure you're okay?"

"My face is half red. What do you think?"

Her mom let out a breath before grabbing her purse and withdrawing her keys. "You sound normal to me. I'll see you tonight for dinner."

"I hope peas aren't on the menu. You might not have any left by then."

Her mother paused by the garage door. "I was thinking of grabbing some take-out since I probably won't have time to cook anything."

Sam brightened. "I can cook dinner." She'd tried to help out a few times since she'd been home, but her sweet, amazing cook of a mother couldn't help but take over when Sam wasn't doing it just right. Her demotion from assistant chef to gopher always happened in a matter of minutes.

Tonight, though, she could be head chef.

Her mother didn't look sold on the idea. "Are you sure? Take-out is fine with me tonight."

"Positive. I'll even whip up some lemon meringue pie for dessert."

"But you've never made lemon meringue."

Oh, but Sam had. Or at least tried. Her roommate had once wanted a lemon meringue pie for her birthday, and Sam had decided it make it herself. It had come out of the oven looking like an overcooked squash. Poor thing.

"I'll learn," said Sam. Tonight would be her chance for redemption. She'd watch several YouTube videos before she even attempted to whip those egg whites. And when she pulled that pie out of the oven later today with all of its stiff, majestic peaks, she could cross yet another thing off her bucket list. Even with a half red face and a few hours of sleep, the rest of the day wasn't looking so bad.

"Where's Dad?"

"He went to the gym with Kevin. Should be back soon, assuming he can still walk."

Sam smiled and gave her mother a dismissive wave. "Off you go, then. I've got peas to defrost, a menu to plan, shopping to do, and a large white chef hat to find."

"Don't forget the apron." Her mother blew a kiss her way. "Thanks, sweetie."

Freshly invigorated, Sam shoved the bag of peas into the freezer and jogged upstairs to get ready for the day. She blew her hair dry and tried her best to tone down the red with foundation, but it made her look like an Oompa Loompa, so she washed it off.

Giving up, she grabbed her phone to search for recipes and found eight new text messages instead.

Five were from her mother.

Where are you?

Your car is still here. Did you go to Emma's?

You're not at Emma's. I just called. Did you fall asleep in your car?

Not in your car, not on the couch. Not in the bathroom. My, you're quiet as a mouse.

Really, where are you?

Two were from Cassie.

11:03 AM: *Want to come to a matinee with the girls and me? Adi's DYING to see you. Starts at 12:30.*

12:28PM: *Guess we'll catch you another time. Have a great day. I want to hear all about your date.*

Sam wrote a quick reply.

Sorry! Didn't get your message until now. Give the girls a kiss from me and bring everyone to dinner tonight. I'm cooking.

The last one was from Colton. Sam's stomach flopped and flipped when she saw his name.

Want to go country dancing tonight?

Sam smiled. Then frowned. Then bit her lip. The thought of spending the evening tucked away in Colton's arms sent a host of happy ripples through her body, but what would another night with him do to those unchangeable, concrete career goals of hers?

It wouldn't touch them. They were unalterable, irreversible, permanent. They *were*.

Still, maybe it would be better not to go. Sam had crossed country dancing off her list the night she and Kajsa had learned a line dance from YouTube anyway.

Undecided, her thumb hovered over the Reply button for a moment before she switched to the internet browser, going straight to her mother's favorite recipe site. She began scrolling through one recipe idea after another, all of them blurring into something resembling mashed potatoes. Her thoughts were too fixated on Colton to concentrate on anything else.

Without even waiting a day, he'd asked her out again. That had to mean he had a great time too. Perhaps even a possible-life-altering good time like she'd had?

No. Guys weren't nearly as dramatic.

Should I? Shouldn't I? Should I? Shouldn't I?

Where was a daisy when she needed one? A Magic 8 ball would work too.

Argh. What was she thinking? Sam had a brain. She was an adult. She could weigh the pros and cons, along with the possible risks, and make this decision on her own.

Maybe she should start a list.

No! No more lists! Enough with the lists!

Her eyes drifted from her phone to her bookcase. On the second shelf, three books from the left, rested her journal.

That was the problem. Right there. Why she couldn't focus. Why she couldn't sleep. Why her brain was a whirling twister. She needed to get away from it.

Be gone, journal, Sam thought as she scampered into the hall. *Be gone.*

She jogged down the stairs, still clutching her phone, and found her father with a large red bowl filled to the brim with Frosted Flakes and milk.

He wrapped an arm protectively around it and pulled it closer to him. "I worked out," he said. "This kind of food is allowed after what Kevin just put me through."

"Don't worry. Mom's not here." Sam picked up the half empty cereal box. "I didn't know she bought sugar cereal anymore. Where did you find this?"

"I picked it up on my way home, along with some other contraband." He nodded toward a grocery sack on the chair next to him. "Want some?"

Realizing she hadn't eaten all morning, Sam nodded. "Don't mind if I do." She filled a regular-sized bowl and took a seat next to her father.

He continued to munch on his cereal as he eyed her.

"What are you doing home? You're usually off gallivanting around the ranch or with Kajsa and Adi.

"Guess all of that 'gallivanting' finally caught up to me because I slept in. But guess what? Mom agreed to let me make dinner tonight. Any suggestions?"

He lifted an eyebrow. "She didn't give you any restrictions on food, the color of vegetables required, or a maximum number of calories allowed?"

"She was in a hurry."

One side of his mouth lifted into a devious smile. "In that case, pasta with the creamiest sauce you can find. The more butter and cream the better. Oh, and French bread too, slathered in butter and garlic and Parmesan cheese."

Sam nodded, thinking about a yummy white sauce her roommate used to make with yogurt. When it came to her father's health, she was okay with letting a few "contraband" items sneak past, but there was a limit to what she'd do for her dad. Hopefully, he wouldn't notice or would chalk it up to Sam's subpar cooking abilities.

"Pasta and white sauce it is."

"Oh, and dessert."

"I'm making lemon meringue."

"Perfect." He shoved another spoon of sugar-coated flakes in his mouth. "What am I going to do when you leave me for New York?"

Sam took a small bite of her own cereal and studied her father. "You're okay with me going, right? I mean, you wouldn't really want me to turn down the job to stay here, would you?"

"Are you kidding? Opportunities like that don't come along every day. I know your mother gives you a hard time about leaving, but that's only because she's going to miss you. *We're* going to miss you. But *we're* excited for you too. In fact, I've already caught her looking at airline tickets to New York."

"Really?" That was news to Sam. Great news. It meant that her mother had faith that her daughter really would stick to her career convictions despite a certain distraction named Colton McCoy.

If only Sam had as much faith in herself.

"Have the time of your life in New York," said her dad. "Work hard for Jason Brecken, go to as many shows as you can, see the sights, and enjoy the adventure of it all. Just keep making good choices and don't forget who you are."

"Never."

"I know. But parents are obligated to say that every once in a while."

"Thanks, Dad."

Sam finished her cereal and rinsed her bowl in the sink. Then she turned around, leaned her hip against the sink, and folded her arms. "Dad, can I get your advice about something?"

"Considering I'm the wisest person I know, you should always get my advice."

She shifted positions, digging her toes into the rug on the floor in front of the sink. "Well, I'm going to New York, right? I mean, *going*. As in there's-absolutely-no-way-I'd-ever-change-my-mind going."

"I didn't realize I was trying to change your mind."

"I know. It's just that Colton . . ." This was harder to explain than Sam thought.

"*Colton's* trying to change your mind?"

"No, of course not," she said quickly. "We haven't talked about the future yet. I mean, who has a DTR after only one date?"

"Then what's the problem?"

"It's that list—that *stupid* list Mom made me start when I was sixteen. It's messing with my head and making me think about things I shouldn't be thinking about yet. One date, Dad! One! Well, possibly two if I go dancing with him

121

tonight. Which is exactly the problem because I don't know if it should be two even though I really want it to be. And Colton—well, he's special and different enough to make me worry that maybe it shouldn't be two because it might mess with everything. You know? And now I have no idea what to do."

Her father squeezed the bridge of his nose, as though he felt a headache coming on. "I'm sorry, sweetie, but would you mind translating that into English?"

"I thought you were wise."

"Not when it comes to gibberish."

With a sigh, Sam walked back to the table and plopped down, resting her arms on top. "I like Colton. A lot."

He nodded. "I gathered that much."

"I want to keep dating him, but I'm worried that if I do, he might make me forget about my goals and keep me here. And I don't want to forget about my goals. So it's better to stop dating him now, right? If we keep going out, my life is only going to get more and more complicated, and who wants a complicated life?"

Her dad pushed the large bowl aside and dropped his chin to the top of his clasped fingers. "Honey, no matter what direction you take in your life, there will always be forks in the road. There might even be roundabouts with lots of different options. Sometimes you can see where a road will go without having to drive down it, and other times, it disappears around a bend and you have to go a ways before you know where it'll take you. Colton sounds like that kind of road. Maybe he'll be a part of your future and maybe he won't. You won't know if you don't give it a try."

"But—"

"I'm not saying that you should forget New York. All I'm saying is that even if you give Colton a chance and he becomes more special and—different, was it?—you can still go to New York. Only instead of a destination, maybe it'll just be a detour on your way back here."

Sam let her father's words sink in. As she did, a calm and peaceful feeling settled around her like a large bean bag chair. He was right. So, beautifully right. She pushed her chair back and threw her arms around her father.

"Thanks, Dad." She kissed his cheek. "Thank you, thank you, thank you."

"So you admit I'm wise."

"The wisest in the land." Her gaze rested on the bag of "contraband" on the counter. "And the sneakiest. If you want a good hiding place for that, I'd stash it at the bottom of the China cabinet in that large bowl Aunt Marinda gave Mom for Christmas a few years ago. She hates it and only keeps it around for the occasional times Aunt Marinda comes to town. She'll never look there."

Her father smiled. "Looks like I passed on some of that brilliant wisdom to you."

"Just don't be surprised if I help myself to your stash on occasion."

"Only if you promise to leave the Peachie-Os alone."

"Deal." She snatched her phone and reopened Colton's text, ready to respond now.

SAM: *I'm in. But only if you come to dinner first. I'm cooking tonight and lemon meringue might be on the menu.*

COLTON: *Sounds risky. Want some help?*

SAM: *Warning: My parents will be here. Maybe even the Mackies and Granthams. Still want to come?*

COLTON: *The more the merrier. The Mackies already love me.*

SAM: *As do my parents.*

COLTON: *Sweet. Seven down. Two to go.*

SAM: *Who's the seventh?*

COLTON: *You . . . right?*

SAM: *Definitely. But you forgot the twins, so four to go. Good luck winning them over. They pull hair, scratch, and steal food.*

COLTON: *Bring it. See you soon.*

Sam smiled at the phone. She'd only just turned down this road, but the view was already lovely.

Fourteen

COLTON RANG THE doorbell and scuffed his Vans against the doormat. Even though they were a few years old, they still looked almost new. That's how often he traded in his boots for regular shoes. Samantha had texted him an hour earlier saying that everyone was coming, so come prepared for a pick-up game of kickball or soccer. Cowboy boots and hats didn't work so well on a playing field, so he'd left both on the passenger seat in his truck, ready to throw on later.

The door opened, and Sam appeared in a breathless frazzle. She wore a green and white polka-dot apron that had been dusted in flour, and there were a few smudges on both of her cheeks—one bright red, the other not so much.

"Wow. You look like a half-ripe tomato after a snowstorm. What happened?"

Her palms flew to her face as though she'd forgotten about the burn. "I fell asleep in the hammock, and—" A beeping sounded from somewhere inside the house, and she turned and ran back the way she'd come, her bare feet leaving a dusty trail across the dark wood floors.

"Come on in," she called over her shoulder.

Colton followed the path of footprints to the kitchen, where he found Sam standing in front of an open oven, her expression a mixture of confusion and distress. The house smelled like lemons and sugar cookies.

"What happened?" she cried, jabbing a finger at whatever baked inside. "I did everything the website said I should do. I made sure there was no yolk in the egg whites, I whipped it until it was stiff, and it's not a humid day. It should have worked. Why didn't it work?"

Colton had no idea. He'd never attempted to make anything involving meringue. But the kitchen already felt like the inside of a barn on a warm summer's day, and the open oven door wasn't helping. So he grabbed a flowery hot pad and removed two shriveled pies from the oven, dropping them on top of the counter before slamming the door closed again.

"They're not supposed to weep or shrink." Samantha glared at the pies as though they were to blame.

"Weep?"

She pointed to small puddles that looked like melted butter. "That's called weeping, and it's a problem."

Before now, Colton had no idea pies could cry.

"I don't understand what happened. I followed the instructions perfectly. And I mean *perfectly*. Do you have any idea how long those took me to make?"

Judging from the way the kitchen looked, with various ingredients scattered around and flour everywhere, Colton assumed a long time. He watched her nervously. "Are you going to weep too?"

Her eyes narrowed—at him this time. "No, I'm not going to weep. I'm going to take those stupid pies and throw them at . . . something."

"As long as that 'something' isn't me." He offered a sympathetic smile. "If it makes you feel any better, it smells amazing in here. They probably still taste good."

Sam leaned against the counter and let out a breath. "This day isn't going very well. Half of my face is sunburned, the kitchen is a wreck, and now I have no lemon meringue pie for dessert. I promised everyone lemon meringue pie. My dad is going to be so disappointed. It's one of his favorites."

Colton opened a few drawers until he found the silverware, then he grabbed a spoon and scooped up a dollop of pie. He blew on it a few times before shoving it into his mouth. The meringue had a decent flavor, but it tasted like the sugar never dissolved, and it stuck to his tongue like melted taffy.

"It's gritty and sticky too, isn't it?" she said.

"And tasty."

"Liar."

He chuckled and pulled her into a hug, running his fingers up and down her back. Her hair smelled like lemons today. "I happen to know how to make a different kind of pie," he said.

"Does it involve homemade crust or egg whites? If so, no thanks."

"It involves one of those pre-made Oreo crusts, mint chocolate chip ice cream, hot fudge topping, and whipped cream."

She pulled back to look at him. "That sounds good."

"It is." His hands continued to travel up and down her arms. "I could run to the store, be back in ten, and have it in your freezer in twenty. What do you think of that?"

"That you're my knight in shining armor. Where have you been my whole life?"

He smiled, and his thumb removed some flour from the unburned side of her face. He wondered if her lips would taste like lemon too. "Do me a favor, will you? The next time you decide to take a nap outside, put up an umbrella first. This looks like it hurts."

"It does." She brushed some flour off the front of his shirt. "Now I've made you all dusty. Sorry."

"If there's one thing I've learned from living on a ranch, it's that I clean up just fine."

"Yes, you do." Her gaze rose from his chest to his face. "Very fine."

It wasn't the first time a woman had said something like that to him, but coming from Samantha the words sounded honest and sincere, like a genuine compliment imbedded in playful banter.

Unable to resist, Colton gave her a light kiss on the forehead. "Be back in ten."

He was back in twelve. She informed him of that the moment she opened her door. She still wore the polka-dotted apron, but there was no trace of flour anywhere—not on the floor, not on the kitchen counter, and not on her. It was like she'd wiggled her nose or snapped her fingers and everything went back to its rightful place. The only evidence that lemon meringue pies had been made in this kitchen was the lingering smell.

"How did you clean up so fast?" He set the grocery bags on the counter. "Do you have little mice helpers hidden somewhere?"

She shuddered. "You're the one with the mice, and from what I could tell, they weren't very helpful."

Colton laughed. "No, they weren't. Still aren't."

She shuddered again.

"Is that why you haven't dropped by since I've moved in?"

"No." She grabbed a bag of what looked like marinated chicken out of the fridge and set it on the counter. "I haven't dropped by because I haven't been invited."

"You don't need an invitation. You're family."

Standing in front of the pantry, she looked over her shoulder. A slight frown marred her expression. "You mean like a sister?"

His lips twitched. "No, not like a sister."

She nodded and returned to her perusal of the pantry. "Good. Because what I feel for you is definitely not sisterly."

She said it in a no-big-deal way, like she'd just made a comment about the weather or a Rocky's game. But Colton suddenly became very interested at the turn this conversation was taking. He moved to stand behind her, letting his hands find her waist. "How do you feel about me, exactly? Motherly?"

Her body stiffened, and her blond curls swayed with the shake of her head.

"Grandmotherly?" he guessed again, leaning over her shoulder so he could see her profile.

"No," came her breathy reply.

"Then what?"

She turned around, clutching a box of pasta like a shield in front of her heart. In her beautiful green eyes, he saw something he'd never seen on her before—uncertainty. The pasta box rose and fell against her chest.

"I feel . . . smitten," she said finally.

Colton's heart began to pound, harder and harder, and the too-warm kitchen became a tropical paradise. Slowly, he took the pasta and set it on the counter to the side of her. Then he re-captured her waist. The fingers of her right hand closed around the baubles on her silver necklace while her left hand fiddled at her side. His gaze was drawn to the exposed skin at the nape of her neck and her lovely collar bone, then rose to her full lips and striking eyes.

"Are you nervous?" he asked.

"Yes."

"Why?"

"Aren't you?"

He didn't answer, but his heart continued to pound. This wasn't his first kiss or his second or even his tenth. He wasn't a novice who didn't know what to do or where to go from here, and yet he'd never been more petrified to act. This went beyond playful experimentation and into something that really mattered. It felt as though his world teetered above him, wobbling in a precarious hold. One word, one move, one touch and everything would either collapse around him or . . .

"It's crazy, right? That I'm nervous." Samantha's voice was as shaky as her fingers. "I mean, it's only been three weeks. We're still in that having fun, getting-to-know-each-other phase. This shouldn't feel this big yet—this . . . monumental, you know? It should still feel light and fun and—"

"Samantha."

"What?"

"Know what my Daddy always says?"

Her head shook again.

"Never miss a good chance to shut up."

She swallowed. "I'm shutting up."

He leaned in slowly and his mouth hovered over hers long enough to smell the lemon on her breath. Then his lips pressed lightly against hers. He tasted something sweet and not sour at all. Her arms wound around his back, pressing against his shoulders, and her body melted against his. The too-warm kitchen became an inferno.

It went against the grain for Colton to move this fast, or to kiss her like this so soon. All his life he'd been taught to tread lightly and carefully. Good things come to those who wait, his father had reminded him over and over again, whenever he'd reached the limit of his patience with an animal, a friend, or his brothers. The night after Colton's first break-up, his father had said it again, reminding Colton that it had taken two years to woo his wife.

Be patient. Give it a little more time. Just wait. Nothing good comes in a hurry.

And then Samantha zipped into his life, stirring up feelings the way her car stirred up dust on the lane.

It's too soon! You're going to regret it! his thoughts maydayed the warning. But Colton didn't want to listen.

Wasn't patience about waiting on someone else's timeline? If a horse was ready to let you ride, you rode. If a brother was begging for a lesson in manners, you taught. And if a girl was ready to be kissed, you complied.

And boy was he complying. His mouth moved right along with hers, and she responded, clinging to him with refreshing, open honesty, holding nothing back.

Maybe that was the difference. Samantha had never held anything back. There was no patiently waiting for her to open up. No need to gradually gain her trust. With her, you didn't need to earn it. She gave it willingly. All Colton had to do was keep it.

"I see you skipped dinner and went straight to dessert," a deep voice intruded.

Colton sprang back and met the unwavering gaze of Samantha's father. Oh boy. Nothing like making a great second impression.

Samantha recovered first. She smoothed her fingers down her apron and cleared her throat. "Hey, Dad. I thought you were helping Kevin with his sprinklers."

"All fixed." He held up two muddy palms to show that he had, indeed, been working in the dirt. "They're running right now if you two need to, uh . . . cool off."

Colton felt the sudden urge to scratch his neck. Samantha, on the other hand, laughed.

"Oh, stop it, Dad," she said. "I guarantee you kissed your fair share of ladies back in the day."

"I might have, but good luck proving it. I never got caught."

"Maybe not kissing," quipped Samantha. "But Mom's not going to be happy when she sees that." She gestured to a trail of muddy footprints her father had left behind.

He looked down at his feet and quickly removed his shoes. "Tell you what," he said. "I'll keep this little . . . episode between the three of us if you clean that up for me."

"Only if you throw in that bag of Peachie-Os."

Her father pointed a finger at her. "Don't push it. It's not easy to get contraband inside this house."

"Fine." She waved a hand at him. "Go get cleaned up, and I'll mop the floor. Again."

He started up the stairs then paused, looking from Colton to his daughter. "No more shenanigans while I'm gone. Got it?"

"Yes, sir," answered Colton.

"We promise to wait until you get back," said Samantha.

Colton tried to hold back his chuckle while her father rolled his eyes and muttered something about how she got her cheekiness from her mother.

As soon as he disappeared, Samantha pointed her finger at Colton and attempted to imitate her father. "No more shenanigans."

"Why didn't you tell me your dad was across the street and could walk in on us any second?"

"Because then you wouldn't have kissed me." She reached around him to grab the box of pasta off the counter. "And I wanted you to kiss me."

"I still would have kissed you. Just . . . not until later."

She smiled and rose up to her tiptoes, giving him a light peck on the lips. "Now's always better. But I'll take later too."

His lips tingling, Colton had to fight the temptation to grab her waist and pull her back into his arms. He felt an undoing of all the years he'd worked so hard to learn patience. One kiss, and he'd hopped on board the Right Here, Right Now wagon.

"Just so you know . . ." She paused by the sink, the uncertainty back in her eyes. "I made a promise to my mom a long time ago that kissing is as far as I'll go before I say 'I do.'" She hesitated, twisting a dishrag around her fingers. "I just . . . wanted you to know up front because a few guys I dated weren't too happy with me when it came out later."

Colton studied her for a moment, wondering how anyone could not be happy with Samantha. She had some sort of inner brightness that lightened everything around her and everyone who came in contact with her. The sun could go down, the lights could go out, but darkness didn't exist near Samantha.

With his hands in his pockets, he moved forward and pressed a soft kiss to her cheek. "Then they were jerks," he whispered.

The uncertainty disappeared and light filled her eyes. "They *were* jerks."

She had never looked more kissable, and Colton would have caved to temptation if he didn't hear footsteps coming from the floor above. He forced his feet to take a few steps back and dragged his gaze to the bag of groceries. "We should probably get those pies made before the ice cream completely liquefies."

"Oh, right."

They spent the next hour making grasshopper pies, grilling chicken, chopping vegetables, cooking a creamy sauce, boiling pasta noodles, tossing a salad, slathering butter and spices on French bread, and finding any excuse to touch, sidle up next to each other, steal a few quick pecks.

At some point, her father trotted back down the stairs, freshly showered, and added more butter to the bread. The Mackies showed up next, with two excited little girls who couldn't wait to tell Samantha and Colton all about the movie they'd seen. Then came the Granthams, followed close behind by Sam's mom.

The bread came out of the oven, all toasted and glistening with butter, and Sam declared, "Let's eat!"

Right away, Colton felt comfortable. He managed to win over the twins by tossing them in the air. They giggled and smiled and wiped gooey fingers all over his shirt, but he didn't care. As he told Emma after her fifth apology: Shirts wash, people wash, and not-so-little babies wash. It's all good.

The kickball game started, and Samantha managed to talk her way out of getting tagged out on first.

Colton rolled his eyes from the pitching mound and called to Kevin, who was manning first, "You're seriously going to let her use the twins as an excuse for taking her time getting to first?"

"What can I say?" Kevin shrugged. "They're adorable kids. Anyone would be distracted by them."

"She's playing you, man."

He tipped his baseball cap at Samantha and said, "Well played."

Samantha grinned in a triumphant way, remaining on first base, and Colton shook his head. The woman had everyone wrapped around her finger.

Eventually, Colton slid into home plate and came away with a nice grass stain up the side of his jeans. But when Kajsa and Adi tackled him because they'd just won the game, it made it all worth it. When it came time for everyone to head home, they hugged him goodbye like he was already part of the family, and as Colton watched them leave, he realized that the only place he'd felt more at home was at home.

Samantha closed the front door and collapsed against it, eyeing him up and down. "I'm not sure we're in the best condition to go country dancing. What do you say we snuggle in the hammock instead?"

There was only one problem. "How will your parents feel about that?" Colton asked, nodding in the direction of the kitchen where her parents were still cleaning up.

"Let's go see." She grabbed his hand and pulled him down the hall.

Colton dragged his feet, thinking he didn't feel that "at home" yet.

"We're going outside to snuggle in the hammock," Samantha announced.

Her parents looked up from rinsing and loading the dishes. "Thanks for dinner," said Mrs. Kinsey. "It was really great. And Colton, that grasshopper pie was yummy."

"I concur," said Mr. Kinsey. "We'll have to make that more often."

Mrs. Kinsey gave his arm a pat. "Sorry, honey, but after tonight it's back to green beans and spinach for you. Tonight, I made an exception because Sam and Colton cooked."

"I think it's okay to make exceptions a little more often."

"Not until . . ."

Samantha took the opportunity to pull Colton toward the back door. He followed, thinking, *Wow, that was easy.*

"Hey," Mr. Kinsey's voice called out the moment Samantha slid the door open. "No shenanigans," he was pointing again, looking directly at Colton.

"No, sir."

"Have a good night you two," Mrs. Kinsey called.

Samantha led him to the oversized hammock, and Colton rolled into it, opening his arm to her. She snuggled up beside him, resting her head on his chest. Her hair still smelled like lemons, and Colton combed his fingers through the soft mass of curls.

"I'm really glad you came today," Samantha said.

"Me too." Colton wondered what it would be like to spend every day with Samantha. Train horses with her watching from the fence, ride with her, cook with her, clean with her, and end every day like this, with her curled against him.

He could get used to a life like that.

"I'm going to miss you," she murmured, sounding like she was going to fall asleep any moment.

Miss me? Colton frowned. "Are you going somewhere?"

"Yes, I'm . . ." The sleepiness left her voice, and she lifted her head, looking him in the eyes. "You don't know."

"Know what?"

Her eyes clouded with a mixture of worry and surprise. "My job—the one that doesn't start until the end of summer." A pause. "It's in New York."

Colton felt like someone had jabbed needles into his lungs, draining them of air. New York? She was leaving? For good? His fingers stilled in her hair. "I didn't know."

"Kajsa didn't tell you." It was more of a statement than a question.

"I'm pretty sure I would have remembered if she had." Colton pulled his arm out from under her and swung around into a seated position, making Samantha pull her knees to her chest. His feet scuffed against the stamped concrete, and he stared at the dark crevices of the patterns, seeing a map of the US with New York on one side and Colorado closer to the other.

Samantha grabbed his arm. "I'm so sorry. Kajsa has told you everything else. I just assumed that—"

"I didn't know," he repeated, not knowing what else to say. It was the truth. He had no idea that Samantha would be packing her bags for a cross country move in only two short months. He'd assumed the graphic design job was here or at the very least, Denver. That was a doable commute. But New York? Not so much.

No good thing comes in a hurry, the thought returned to his mind like a rude I-told-you-so, sticking out its tongue and making a face.

Colton felt a stab of regret. Why had he asked her out? And why the heck had he kissed her? He should have kept things between them as friends and let them eventually gravitate toward acquaintances and then distant acquaintances, which is what would have happened if he hadn't jumped the gun.

If only he'd known. If only Kajsa had clued him in on that tiny detail. Actually, why hadn't Samantha? All along, she'd known. She'd flirted, gone out with him, and kissed him back. She'd made him feel like a future could exist between them. Why?

And then Colton remembered her stupid bucket list and a large lump lodged in his throat. "I'm your summer fling, aren't I?"

"What? No." Her fingers tightened around his arm. "Colton, I—"

He pulled his arm free and stood, turning around to look down at her. "Samantha, if I'd known you were moving to New York in August, I wouldn't have asked you out or even flirted with you. I told you before, and I'll tell you again. I don't do flings." His jaw tightened. "At least I didn't before now."

The light was still on inside, so Colton headed for the side of the house. Behind him, Samantha's footsteps followed.

"Colton, wait. It isn't like that. Can we please talk about this?"

He paused with his hand on the latch and looked over his shoulder. "Say we keep dating. Is New York negotiable?"

From the look on her face, Colton knew her answer before she said it. "I can't turn down this job. I just can't. It's too—"

"Congratulations," he cut her off. "You just crossed another item off your bucket list." Then he shoved the gate open, strode to his truck, jumped inside, and didn't look back as he took off down the road. He'd been wrong about darkness not existing around Samantha. Right now, his world had never felt so black.

Fifteen

SAM LAY IN the hammock alone, watching the few stars that could be seen. Sleeping beneath the stars wasn't supposed to feel like this. It was supposed to be peaceful, adventurous, romantic. Not . . . blah. How she hated feeling blah.

At least I didn't get too far down the Colton road before turning back.

At least . . .

Sam couldn't think anymore. She rolled to her unburned side and curled into a ball, trying not to think about Colton or the way it had felt to be kissed and held by him. The way it had felt to watch him walk away. Over the past few years, she'd kissed her fair share of guys, but none of them, no matter how good or practiced they were, came close to getting into her soul the way Colton had so easily done.

But now he was gone, and Sam felt bereft, like something valuable and precious had been taken from her grasp—something that never belonged to her in the first place.

Why couldn't her job start tomorrow? Why couldn't she pack her bags, hop on a plane, and leave all this aching blahness behind? She'd once thought a summer without Kajsa and Adi would be bad, but that was nothing compared to the oppressive feeling that dimmed everything, including the stars.

The truth was, Samantha didn't want to pack her bags or hop on a plane anytime soon. Nor did she want to go back in time and undo the past couple of weeks. She wanted to continue forward down the Colton road and keep seeing those glimpses of a possible life that took her breath away. A life that made her believe in The List.

Up until now, Sam had thought Colton's arrival in her life was bad timing. But maybe it wasn't. Maybe it was a sign that New York shouldn't be a detour on her way back to Colorado Springs. Maybe it was a road that shouldn't be travelled at all.

The back door slid open and light footsteps padded across the patio.

"Sam?" A dark shadow in the form of her mother's head peered down at her. "I heard Colton's truck leave a while ago. What are you still doing out here?"

Sam rolled to her back, feeling a renewed sense of blah. Maybe her mother could shoo it away. "He found out about New York and said he doesn't do flings. So he left."

Her mother was silent for a moment. "I see."

Those two words, spoken so quietly, became Sam's undoing. Tears welled up in Sam's eyes, her fingers balled into fists, and she hit the hammock in frustration. She hated crying even more than she hated feeling blah. She hated it so much she'd made a pact to herself long ago that she'd never cry again.

So much for pacts and bucket lists and career goals and The List. As far as she was concerned, they'd all just crumbled.

"He wasn't a fling." The words shook, giving away her tears.

Her mother crawled into the hammock and put her arm around Sam, hugging her close. "I know," she whispered. "I know."

Sam had been hurt by guys before, but she'd never felt it so deeply inside of her. Like someone had just vacuum-packed her soul, shriveling her heart into a tiny ball, like an over-dried raisin.

Real heartbreak sucked.

"Give him some time. Then you can explain."

"Explain what?" said Sam. "That I'm still leaving and want him to wait for me? Or that I'm willing to give up an opportunity I've worked so hard for to stay here?"

Her mother lifted her head. "Are you willing to give it up?"

Sam wiped her nose with the back of her hand. "I don't know. I just know the thought of losing him hurts worse than losing the job." Sam sniffed. "That should make you happy."

The dark, now-blurry head shook slowly. "No, sweetie, it doesn't. Yes, it's been hard to watch you grow up and begin to spread your wings, and yes, I would have loved your dream job to be here instead of Manhattan. But what I care most about is your happiness. You've always been so driven, so sure of yourself, and I've always been so proud." Her mom stroked her hair. "If you're not happy, how could I possibly be?"

Sam turned into her mother, holding her tight. "I feel like I have to choose between them, and I don't want to choose. I want them both."

A cricket filled the silence with a relaxed *cricken . . . cricken . . . cricken*, as though it had no other care in the world. How nice would it be to lounge in this hammock with no worries, no cares, no fears? No thought beyond the sound of the crickets, the rustle of leaves, or the swing and sway of the hammock.

"Have you asked him what *he* wants?"

"No." Sam swallowed. "He left without really hearing me out."

"It's not easy to listen when you're hurting."

"I know."

"Give him a few days," her mother encouraged. "Then see if he gives you a real reason to cry. But my guess is he won't."

The stars high above seemed to brighten as though the dimmer switch slid up a notch. Sam breathed in a wisp of hope and a hint of the neighbor's lilac bush. Sam swiped the back of her hand across her eyes, clearing away the tears. Her mother was right. The heartache, the worry, the stress—it was all premature. Someday, they might trouble her again, but not yet.

Not yet.

Colton tossed the saddle on the mustang's back and began to tighten it. "You don't have an audience today, Maj, but you'd still better behave. I'm in no mood to get tossed in the dirt."

The horse's answering sniff sounded like a retort.

"I mean it. If you throw me, no oats or carrots for an entire week."

Colton yanked hard on the strap, grabbed the reins, and swung onto Maj's back. Other than smacking the soft earth of the corral with her front right hoof, the horse made no move to unseat her rider.

Huh. Maybe all the horse needed was a good talking to—someone to lay down the law. Colton tsked and urged the horse forward with the heels of his boots, but Maj didn't budge. Like a stubborn mule, she simply stood there, playing with the bit in her mouth. Colton tried again, this time tapping a little harder and tsking louder. Still no movement.

"Unbelievable," he muttered as he slid from the horse. Moving to the front, he tugged on the reins, trying to coerce Maj forward, but the horse stayed rooted. If she could talk, she probably would have said, "No audience, no ride. Deal with it."

Colton was through dealing with it. "Fine. You don't want to be trained, don't be trained. Just don't blame me when you end up back in some miserable federal holding facility because nobody wants a horse with an ego the size of Jupiter."

A light buzz of an engine sounded, growing louder and louder until a beefy, camo-colored 4-wheeler appeared around the bend, speeding toward the house. Colton sighed. Under normal circumstances, he'd be glad to see his friend. But today, he wasn't in the mood.

Will careened toward him, then slammed on the brakes and skidded to a stop just outside the gate. He killed the engine and pulled the helmet off his head, revealing a sweaty mop of sandy, curly hair.

"So you're back," said Colton. Not long after they'd returned from the mustang roundup, Will had taken off on another. And another. He was trying to save up for his last year of college, and the roundups paid pretty well. If Colton didn't have a problem seeing wild animals being taken from their natural habitat, he would have done the same.

"I'm back." Will leapt off the 4-wheeler and approached Colton, eyeing Maj with a grin. "How's she doing?"

"Now that you're here? Probably better than a few minutes ago."

Will laughed. "I do have a certain animal magnetism about me, don't I?"

Colton mounted again and urged the horse forward once more. When she began walking, he rolled his eyes.

"Don't flatter yourself. Maj isn't picky about who's watching, only that someone is. And the more, the merrier."

"Maj?" Will asked, his left eyebrow lifting. "What kind of name is that?"

"Short for Your Majesty."

Will threw back his head and laughed. "Who came up with that one?"

"I did." Kajsa stood on the front porch with her hand on her hips, glaring at Will, who stopped laughing immediately.

"Sorry, Kaj. But you have to admit, it's kind of a funny name."

Kajsa climbed the fence next to Will and leaned forward, stroking Maj's nose. "It fits you perfectly, doesn't it, Your Majesty?" she cooed. The horse practically preened with the attention.

Before he could stop himself, Colton's gaze swept the drive, looking for signs of a yellow Bug. "When did you get here?" he asked Kajsa.

"Cassie had a doctor's appointment in Denver, so she dropped me off early. Adi too. We've been helping your mom paint your old room."

"My room?" Colton had no idea his room was getting a facelift. "Why?"

Adi emerged from the house and walked to the front porch railing. "She's turning it into a guest room," she answered.

Now that Colton was paying attention, he could see that both girls were dotted with paint, but with the sun glinting off the windows behind them, he couldn't tell what color it was. Only that it was light.

"Did you move out?" Will asked Colton. "Or did they finally get sick of your sorry hide and kick you out?"

"I moved to The Shack," said Colton. "What color are you painting it?"

"Yellow."

"Yellow?" He frowned, picturing his masculine room

becoming a bright, feminine shade of yellow—his least favorite color at the moment. Any color with a hint of yellow in it could get dumped into the Pacific for all he cared. What was so wrong with the formerly gray walls?

"It's the color of Sam's car," said Adi, lifting her arm to show him the speckles of paint. "Me and Kajsa picked it out because we thought you'd like it."

Colton stifled a groan. This is exactly why he would never again date anyone who knew his family or Kajsa's family or even Will's family. From now on, he'd meet all girls via the internet and only bring home a woman once he'd put a ring on her finger. What was his mom thinking to let them paint that room yellow?

"I am so lost right now," said Will.

"Colton's dating Sam," said Adi with a sly grin.

"Sam?" Will's brow arched.

"Sam is short for Samantha," Colton said.

"Adi! Kajsa!" his mother's voice called from somewhere inside the house. "Where are you girls?"

"Coming!" Giving one last pat to Maj, Kajsa followed her sister inside.

Will turned toward Colton, folding his long arms over the top of the fence, and gave him a considering look. "Since when did you move out and start dating someone? I haven't been gone that long."

Colton tried to urge the horse forward, but this time, even with Will standing there, Maj refused to budge. "We aren't dating."

"Maybe you should tell Adi and Kajsa that." Will nodded in their direction. "Preferably before they finish painting."

"It's complicated."

"Why?"

"Because Samantha is their favorite person, and if I tell them we aren't dating anymore . . . well, they won't understand."

"So what, you're going to keep dating some chick because you don't have the heart to tell the girls you're not interested any longer?"

"I am interested." Colton kicked Maj's flank again, only to grind his teeth in frustration when she didn't move.

Will was silent for a moment, probably trying to make sense of it all. "Oh, I get it. She broke up with *you*." A grin followed his epiphany. "Wow. Has that ever happened to you before?"

"Nobody broke up with anybody. Like I said, we weren't really dating."

"What does that even mean? Did you make a move on her or not?"

This was exactly why Colton wasn't thrilled to see Will roll up the drive. The guy could be annoying and infuriating and he always stuck his nose where it didn't belong. When Maj still wouldn't move, Colton jumped to the ground and began removing the saddle. He had better things to do than play twenty questions with his friend and get nowhere with the world's most stubborn animal.

Will gave a little whoop and a laugh. "You *did*."

"It's over, okay? *Over*. She's moving to New York at the end of the summer and that's that."

"How can it be over when summer's not over? You could have a lot of fun during the next two months."

Colton felt his last thread of patience stretch to the point of breaking. "Like I told her—I don't do flings."

Will's grin widened further. "Oh, wow. You really like this girl." He slapped the top of the fence and laughed. "Well, whadoyaknow, the great Colton McCoy has finally fallen."

Colton didn't think his mood could get any darker that morning, but if Will kept going on like this, thunderclouds would be rolling in any second. He didn't want to hear about yellow rooms or sunny skies or Samantha. He didn't want Will stirring the pot or playing Sherlock. All he wanted was for Maj to do what she was told without an audience for once.

"Just drop it, Will." Colton tossed the saddle over the fence and removed the bridle, throwing it on top. "Don't you have someplace you need to be right now?"

"Sorry, bro. Didn't meant to hit a nerve." Instead of climbing back on his ATV and leaving Colton alone, Will lingered. "If you really don't want this girl to leave then why not give her a reason to stay? Since when have you ever given up without a fight?"

Colton paused by the fence, looking over the top of the well-used, leather saddle toward the barn. He'd given up because Samantha had said New York wasn't negotiable, but did that mean it really wasn't? *Had* he given up without a fight? Was there a chance Samantha would consider finding a different job instead—say in Colorado?

Colton would never know because he'd put an end to their relationship before it had a chance to begin. He'd gotten hurt, jumped to conclusions, and cut his losses.

Is that how he wanted things to end?

No.

Colton nodded at his friend. "Know what, Will? I'm actually glad you dropped by this morning."

"Glad enough to offer to feed me whatever smells so good?"

Colton sniffed the air, and the scent of fresh-out-of-the-oven blueberry muffins teased his nostrils. How had he not noticed that before? "It's technically not my house anymore, but we should definitely investigate. Just let me put this saddle away."

Will clapped him on the back. "Now you're talking."

Sixteen

THE RUMBLE OF a gas-powered motor blared in Sam's ears as she battled to keep the chainsaw steady enough to cut the large block of ice into the shape of a cowboy boot. It was Kajsa's birthday party tonight, and she planned to make the coolest (no pun intended) centerpiece Kajsa had ever seen. Unfortunately, there was nothing delicate about chainsaw blades—especially one held by shaking hands. By the time she shut off the engine, the boot looked more like something an Eskimo might wear.

Sam removed her safety goggles and studied the L-shaped lump of ice. No matter. She would do the rest by hand. Fishing through her quickly-gathered tools, she grabbed a hammer and a chisel and began pounding away at the ice. Within the hour, she'd turned the Eskimo shoe into something that looked more like a chalk outline of a cowboy boot. She found some sandpaper for smoothing, and after going through several sheets, Sam finally had a decent ice sculpture of a cowboy boot.

All she needed now was Adi. Sam glanced at the time on her phone. She'd invited Adi over to help with the cake and centerpiece while Cassie finished some last-minute shopping, but if she didn't show up soon, the boot would become a puddle.

Five minutes later, the back door slid open, and Adi walked out in a knee-length sunflower sundress, lugging one of Noah's tool cases. She looked beautiful and festive, a stark comparison to Sam's cut-off jean shorts and dampened pink tank.

Sam smiled. "Perfect timing. Is that the Dremel?"

Adi's blonde, curly ponytail bounced as she nodded. "Sorry I'm late. Me and Kajsa helped Aunt Jane paint a room this morning and it took *forever* to get the paint off." She sat the case on the table and examined the ice sculpture. "Wow, that really does look like a boot!"

"You sound surprised. Did you really think that it wouldn't?"

Adi shrugged. "Daddy said you've never sculpted ice before, so I should say something nice no matter how it looked. But it looks so boss! And I'm not just saying that to be nice."

Sam touched the tip of Adi's nose. "So I have your dad to blame for your lack of faith in me. He's lucky he loaned me his Dremel so now I can't be mad at him." Sam opened the box and pulled out a small tool in the shape of a plastic soda bottle. It looked different than the one the artist had used in the YouTube video she watched, but a Dremel was a Dremel, right?

With Adi's help, she figured out how to attach the bit, found an extension cord in the garage, and turned it on. The tool hummed, the bit spun, and Sam grinned at Adi. "What do you say? Should we girl-up this cowboy boot?"

Adi nodded, her eyes bright with excitement.

Using a picture of a boot she'd found online, Sam began drawing decorative designs across the sculpture. After a few minutes, she handed the Dremel to Adi and let her take a turn. Her small hands shook with the vibrations of the tool, and the lines and curves began to look as though they had a mind of their own. It was adorable.

When the boot was covered in lines, circles, flowers, and arcs, the girls carefully moved it to the large freezer in Sam's garage where it would wait until the party. Then they headed inside to decorate the cake. Noah and Cassie's refrigerator had sprung a leak a week earlier, and now a huge section of their kitchen floor was in the process of getting redone, so Cassie had asked if they could have the party in the Kinsey's backyard.

"Is Kajsa still at the ranch?" Sam asked as they slathered turquoise frosting on the bottom tier of the cake.

Adi nodded. "Aunt Jane and Colton are keeping her busy until tonight. She's so excited."

Sam bit her lower lip, wishing she wouldn't have asked the question. Thinking of the ranch made her think of Colton, and she'd been trying her hardest not to go there during the past two days. But even though she'd kept herself busy with a few things on her bucket list—like finding the perfect mascara, attempting to make another lemon meringue pie, and donating blood—thoughts of him constantly took up space at the back of her mind, making her question New York and if it really was where she wanted to be in the fall.

When the bottom tier was finished, they added the top tier and frosted it with a white base layer and turquoise polka-dots. Sam had filled two bags with frosting so they could each do the job.

"Hey, Adi," said Sam, adding another dot, "you know I'm moving to New York at the end of the summer, right?" It was a question that had been bothering her ever since her discussion with Colton the other night. Years ago, when she'd told the girls she'd be leaving for college, they'd had a meltdown. They'd cried and clung to her, saying they didn't want her to leave them. But with the New York job, there had been no crying, no clinging, and no exclamations of missing her. Maybe the reason Kajsa hadn't said anything to Colton was because they didn't know either.

Or maybe they'd grown up enough that they didn't care.

"Yeah, I know," said Adi as though it was old news. Her mouth didn't droop even a little. Ouch.

"Do you know how far away New York is?"

"*Really* far," said Adi. "Daddy said it would take at least three days to drive there." She sounded so nonchalant about the whole thing that Sam's heart began to deflate. Had they outgrown their old babysitter already? Please no.

"Aren't you going to miss me?"

Adi stopped piping and turned her large brown eyes on Sam. "I always miss you when you're gone. But I know you'll be back because you always come back. Cassie said that's what sisters do."

Sisters. The word wrapped around Sam's heart like a fuzzy blanket fresh from the dryer. To the girls, she was no longer the babysitter who would move on and out of their lives. She was their sister. Sam had always wanted a sister. Now she had two.

She threw her arms around her former-charge-turned-sister and pulled her close. "That's right, Adi. I will always come back. I could never stay away from my *sisters* for long."

Adi smiled, and Sam's day brightened.

They finished the cake by trimming the base of both tiers with tan frosting that looked like a rope. The finishing touch was Sam's present to Kajsa. On the top of the cake, she rested a small jewelry box in the shape of a tan cowgirl hat. Inside was a sterling silver horseshoe necklace embedded with tiny, sparkling cubic zirconias. Kajsa wasn't one for jewelry, but Sam hoped, given that it was a horseshoe and a gift from Sam, she'd wear the necklace. It would look adorable on her.

"She's going to love it," said Adi.

"I hope so."

"If not, I'll wear it."

Sam smiled at that. Adi loved necklaces and earrings and bows and all things that had to do with accessorizing. "What do you say we paint our nails while we wait for Cassie to get here with the presents?"

"Only if I can pick out the colors."

"Sure."

By the time Cassie arrived, Sam had green, pink, and orange, neon-colored toenails. Her feet would definitely draw some notice tonight.

The Kinsey house was a flurry of activity when Colton arrived with his family. As they walked up the driveway, he purposefully slowed his steps, gravitating toward the back of the pack. Would Samantha pretend like nothing had happened, or would she do her best to avoid him? Relationships could be so awkward. Why had he gotten all bent out of shape over New York, anyway? If he hadn't, Sam would probably be the one to open the door and greet him with a warm smile and a hug.

Instead, it was Mrs. Kinsey's smile that greeted them. She ushered everyone inside, saying how glad she was that they'd made it. Again, Colton let his parents and brothers move ahead of him. As he passed the entrance to the living room, a hand reached out and yanked him inside, and he suddenly found himself face to face with Samantha with no idea what to say. Her curls were piled on top of her head in an artistic way, and her face was no longer half red. She looked gorgeous. The only thought going through Colton's mind was how much he wanted to pull her close and find out what her lips tasted like today.

Thankfully she was more prepared than him. She held up a piece of paper two inches from his face. "See this?"

The words blurred and made him go cross-eyed, so

Colton took the paper and lowered it. Her summer bucket list came into focus.

"I see it," he said slowly, not sure where she was going.

"Great. Now watch this." She stole it back and walked over to the coffee table where she promptly dipped the corner of the paper into a flame of a candle. It caught fire, and she continued to hold it until the flames neared her fingertips. Then she dropped it on a ceramic plate next to the candle and smoothed her fingers against her gray flowered skirt before facing him again.

"My bucket list is officially no more," she announced, clasping her fingers in front of her. "I don't want to run a triathlon, jump out of a plane, or have a fling anymore."

When she didn't continue, Colton said, "What do you want?" There had been nothing spoken about New York or the end of the summer or anything else that threatened to tear them apart. His heart beat double-time as he waited for her answer.

She approached him, stopping a foot away. "To find out what we might become and go from there." Her eyes reflected uncertainty and worry, but also hope.

Cautiously, Colton reached out, took a hold of her forearms, and pulled her hands apart. Then his fingers slid down to her hands and interlocked with her fingers. "Okay."

"Yeah?"

"Yeah."

She let out a breath. "Good. Because I don't think I can handle living through any more days like the last few have been. If you had any idea—"

"Samantha." He pulled her against him.

"Shutting up."

This time when he kissed her, she tasted like vanilla frosting and smelled like cherry blossoms. Colton was reminded of the summer his mother had hung all the clothes out back, letting them dry in the fresh summer air. He'd been seven at the time and loved running through them, smelling the soap and feeling the soft fabric brush against his face.

That's what Samantha felt like. Soft. Fresh. Breezy. Everything about her was lovely and feminine, the antithesis of his everyday life of dirt, sweat, and the smells of animals. A life without her in it wasn't enough anymore.

New York is a bad idea, he wanted to say. *A horrible idea. Don't go.*

"And here we go again," Mr. Kinsey's voice intruded once again.

Colton immediately released Samantha and stepped away, forcing his gaze to meet her father's.

"You know," Mr. Kinsey said. "In the year and a half I dated Becky, not once did I get caught making out with her. But only a couple weeks into your relationship, I've already caught you twice. Do you need a lesson in discretion?"

Colton shook his head. "No, sir."

"So this won't happen again?"

"No, sir."

A giggle escaped Samantha's mouth, and her father turned to leave. "Dinner's ready."

Before Colton could follow, Samantha rose to her tiptoes and kissed his cheek. "Rain check?" she whispered.

"Definitely." With her hand in his, they walked through the kitchen and into the backyard.

Kajsa oohed and aahed over everything—from the decorations to the presents to the cake. Maxwell continually lunged for the ice sculpture and Georgia managed to pull herself up to the table and grab a fistful of cake before anyone could stop her. When Kajsa read that the McCoys had signed her up for her first legitimate barrel race, she squealed.

"Are you sure I'm ready?" she asked Colton, her new horseshoe necklace glinting in the sun.

"You've been ready for months now. We just wanted to give it to you for your birthday."

Then it was hugs all around. Hugs to her dad and Cassie for her very own saddle, new boots, and some cute plaid tops, hugs to Emma and Kevin for the new art set, complete with drawings of horses for her to color, hugs to Mr. and Mrs. Kinsey for a basket filled with her favorite treats, and hugs to Samantha for the necklace.

"I'll wear it every day," she promised.

"You'd better," said Samantha. "Otherwise, Adi might."

Through a mouthful of turquoise cake, Spencer said, "Dusty was going to sign up for the bronc riding, but he chickened out."

"At least I wasn't afraid to ride a harmless little sheep," Dusty shot back.

"That was over ten years ago," Spencer said. "When are you going to stop bringing it up?"

"When you stop being such a moron."

"You're the moron."

"Will you two please be quiet?" demanded Kajsa. "You promised you wouldn't fight at my party."

"Oh, that wasn't fighting," said Dustin. "That was just a lively discussion between brothers."

Colton's father stopped in front of the buffet table and directed a hard look at his sons. "Those involved in the next 'lively' discussion will get clean-up duty after the party is all over."

That quieted the brothers. But it also gave Colton a good reason to goad them into a "lively" discussion again.

"Remember that time when someone filled your boot with manure, Spence?" said Colton. "You always thought it was Brock, but really it was Dusty."

"What?" spluttered Spence, spewing some remnants of his cake at his brother. "You are so going to pay for that."

Dustin glared at Colton. "Traitor," he mouthed.

Samantha joined in the fun. "Last week, I overheard Spence saying that you looked like a bobble head on the back of a horse, Dusty."

"It's true." Spence chortled. "You bounce all over the place when you ride, like an amateur city boy."

Dustin's jaw clenched, his fist tightened around his fork, and Colton smiled and slung his arm around Samantha's shoulders, leading her away. "That should do it. You can thank me later."

Sure enough, the bickering began anew, and the brothers ended up with a dishrag and broom in their hands.

As the night came to a close, Colton scanned the backyard, listening to the chatter and laughter that filled the space between the fences and beyond. Adi had pitched in to help his brothers clean up, and Georgia and Maxwell sat in highchairs, digging into a pile of mashed-up cake. The light breeze from earlier had turned into more of a gust, quaking the aspens, tossing the helium balloon bouquet, and blowing Sam's curls all around her head.

Colton pulled her close and pressed a kiss to her forehead, thinking how great it felt to be part of the family, how lucky he was to have Samantha at his side, and how determined he was to do whatever it took to keep things this way.

Seventeen

AFTER THE PARTY, Colton became a daily part of Sam's life. She spent most mornings at the ranch, hanging out with him while he worked with Maj, going on a quick ride with him, or helping his mother with lunch or various other projects. When it came time for Kajsa's afternoon lessons, she went home to do something with Adi, watched Maxwell and Georgia for Emma, or spent time with her mom or dad. Then evening rolled around, and she'd see Colton again. They'd get together for dinner at the Kinsey's house, The Shack, or go out for a burger and country dancing or to a movie.

On the Fourth of July, the Mackies, Granthams, and Kinseys all joined the McCoys for a tasty barbeque and homemade ice cream, complete with sparklers. As darkness fell, they gathered together some blankets, climbed into the back of a few pick-ups, and travelled on a bumpy dirt road up the mountain to a clearing where they settled in and watched the spectacular Memorial Park fireworks show. Snuggled under a blanket next to Colton, Sam wanted to stay there forever. That had been a great day.

And so had the others. Sam looked forward to them all, thinking more of Colton and less of New York. But every once in awhile, her thoughts drifted into the murky, uncomfortable territory of her future. She'd already signed a six-month lease on her apartment and sent a check in the amount of her first and last months' rent. If she was going to get out of the contract, she'd have to find someone to take it over soon. Very soon. She also needed to give Brecken Design enough time to find a replacement.

Replacement.

The thought of someone else sitting in the cubicle meant for her scratched at Sam's nerves the way fingernails scratched against an emery board. It didn't feel right. Nothing felt right—neither leaving nor staying.

With her blinds closed and the evening sun beginning to dim, Sam stared at the August calendar on her phone. Besides a friend's birthday on the fifth and National S'mores Day on the tenth, only one other event was scheduled—an event that had been created over three months ago. Lying on her stomach on her bed, Sam tapped on Thursday, August 24, then again on the event scheduled at 10:45 AM.

Flight #4563, Denver to NYC

Time: 10:45AM—8:23PM

Note: Confirmation #7C14X210 (Dreams really come true!!!)

But did dreams really come true? When August twenty-fourth arrived, what would Sam be doing? Would the flight be cancelled and the job turned down? Or would she be shoving the last of her toiletries into a travel bag, tucking that into one of her suitcases, and sitting shotgun while her mother or father drove her to the airport?

Sam dropped the phone on her bed and stared at the ceiling. She thought of what her dad told her, about New York just being a detour, and wondered if maybe she could still have both. But was she willing to risk losing Colton to find out? What if she loved the job at Brecken Design so much that she wanted to stay? What if Colton met someone else while she was away?

What if? What if? What if?

What Sam wouldn't give for a crystal ball right now.

If only Colton could uproot his life and come with her. Then all those what ifs would go away. But he couldn't exactly tie millions of helium balloons to the ranch, carry it to New York and set it down in Central Park. Nor could he leave it behind and start over. What would a cowboy do in Manhattan anyway? Colton would go crazy in a place as congested as New York City. He loved the wide-openness of his ranch too much.

Blowing a few strands of ticklish hair from her face, Sam rolled off her bed and plodded toward her bathroom, stopping next to her dresser. The wooden sign she'd designed over a month ago had finally arrived, and here it sat, waiting for the perfect opportunity to be given to Colton.

Should she give it to him tonight?

As Sam reapplied her mascara, she heard a tap on her bedroom door, followed by her mother's voice. "Knock, knock."

"Who's there?" Sam watched through the mirror as her mom let herself in.

"Becky."

"Becky who?"

"Becky, the mom who never sees her daughter anymore."

Sam leaned in to touch up her eye shadow. "Have you already forgotten we went out to lunch the other day?"

"If by 'other day' you mean last week, you're right. We did. But that café was too loud to hear myself think, and every day since it's been more of a hi and goodbye."

Sam set down her makeup and met her mother's gaze through the mirror. "I'm sorry. Between you, Adi, the twins,

Kajsa, and Colton, I'm feeling a little stretched."

A pensive look appeared in her mother's eyes. "Is that all you're feeling stretched about?"

Sam fiddled with the black mascara tube, thinking how easy inanimate objects had it. They had no minds to think, no questions to ask, no decisions to make. Everything was done for them.

"I wish you could make my decision for me."

Her mom leaned against the counter and cocked her head to the side. "I wouldn't know what to tell you if I could. What feels right?"

"They both do and they both don't. That's the problem. How can two rights make me feel so wrong and confused? Sometimes I wish I'd never gotten the job offer."

Her mom moved behind Sam and combed her fingers through her daughter's hair. Normally, Sam loved it when she did that. It relaxed and soothed her. But today it didn't do any of that. It only frizzed her curls.

"Do you sometimes wish you'd never met Colton too?" her mother asked softly.

"No, I'd never wish that. I'd take him over the job any day of any week of any month. But an amazing opportunity has landed in my lap, and I just can't . . ." Sam's voice trailed off as the inky blackness of indecision and possible regret created a churning mass in her stomach.

"You want both," said her mother.

Sam nodded.

"Have you talked to Colton about it?"

"No. Things are going so well. I don't want to stir the pot."

"Well, honey, the pot is going to need to be stirred sooner or later."

"I'd prefer it be later."

Her mother's hands settled on Sam's shoulders, and she gave them a squeeze. "Things are going to work out no matter what you decide."

It was true. Things always had a way of working out in the long run, but not always without regret. And Sam didn't want any regrets—not major ones anyway. She didn't want to run into a closed door that would have been open if she'd only taken the job. And she *really* didn't want to step aside while someone else walked down the aisle toward Colton. That would be the worst regret of all.

Sam dropped her head, feeling like her thoughts were too heavy to hold any longer. "I need a Magic 8 Ball," she said. "Those things are never wrong, right?"

"Wrong."

"Dang."

Her mother's laugh accompanied the faint sound of the doorbell chiming. "Sounds like Colton is here. What are your plans for tonight?"

Sam shrugged. "I don't know. Just the usual, I guess. Dinner and hanging out and trying to avoid thinking about the future."

"The usual?" Her mother's eyebrow lifted. "The Sam I know would never fill her summer days with 'dinner and hanging out.' She'd fill them with the stuff good memories are made of, don't you think?"

Her mom left to answer the door. Sam, on the other hand, stayed in her bathroom, watching her reflection in the mirror without really seeing it. Her mother was right. She'd let the worry of indecision overshadow her usual enthusiasm and creativity. She'd become a hum-drum, weighted down person who was allowing precious time to pass her by. This wasn't her. She didn't want this to be her.

Sam gave herself a hard look. "You are a spunky, vivacious woman. Don't forget it," she said out loud. Someday soon, she'd figure out what to do with Thursday, August twenty-fourth. In the meantime, she'd make the rest of the days ones to remember.

Sam slipped on her white, strappy sandals, shoved her phone into her large purse, grabbed two beach towels from the hall closet, and trotted down the stairs, leaving the foil-wrapped gift on top of her dresser. She found Colton in the kitchen with her father, tossing some chocolate-covered almonds into his mouth. When he saw her, he smiled.

"Hey, gorgeous. Long time no see."

Sam didn't bother reminding him she'd seen him only that morning. "There's been a change of plans. Instead of going to Drifters for burgers tonight, we're going shopping."

Her father tried to cover up a laugh with a cough while Colton frowned. "Shopping?"

Sam nodded. "You are in some serious need of some non-cowboy clothes. Do you even own sandals?"

He glanced at his jeans and boots. "What's wrong with these?"

Sam exchanged a look with her mother before tugging on Colton's arm. "You can't go fountain hopping wearing that," she said as she pulled him toward the door.

"I'm sorry. Did you just say *fountain hopping*?"

"Yes."

Her excitement was soon deflated when they arrived at the store, and Colton shot down everything she pulled off the rack or pointed out to him.

"Plaid belongs on shirts, not shorts—unless you're a golfer, which I'm not."

A quick look around the store, and Sam spotted a man wearing black plaid shorts and a green t-shirt. "Look." She pointed. "He's wearing plaid, and I guarantee he's not a golfer."

"Excuse me, sir." Colton raised his voice, and the man glanced his way.

"Yes?"

"Do you golf?"

"When I get the chance."

"Thank you." Colton looked back at Sam. "See?"

She rolled her eyes. "He's not golfing *now*."

"Maybe he just left the course and hasn't had time to change."

"Why don't you ask him and find out?" she muttered, placing the shorts back on the rack. She moved on to t-shirts and pulled out a royal blue athletic shirt with a Nike swoosh across the front. "What about this?"

He took the shirt from her hands, and Sam held her breath, hoping she'd finally found something he'd at least be willing to consider. But he promptly hung it back on the rack. "Sorry, but cowboys don't wear silk."

"It's not silk," she said. "It's a combination of spandex, rayon, and polyester. It's an *athletic* shirt. Lightweight, dries easily, and what most guys love about it: doesn't wrinkle."

"It feels like silk. And it's shiny." He lifted an orange cotton t-shirt from another rack and held it up for her inspection. The Denver Bronco's logo stared back. "Now this is a shirt I'll consider."

"It's exactly like every other t-shirt in your closet."

"No. This is orange. I don't have an orange shirt."

"You already have two Bronco shirts that I've seen."

"I actually have three. But this one is *orange*."

She let out a breath of frustration before dragging him over to the shoe department. "What about these?" She pulled a pair of Teva's off the shelf and held them up for his inspection.

He didn't even give them a second look. "Those would be filled with dirt the second I walked out my front door."

Sam replaced them without argument and gestured to his jeans. "Are you really going to wear denim and boots fountain hopping? They'll never dry."

He gnawed on his lower lip before tipping his head to the side. "About this fountain hopping thing . . . have you ever done it before?"

"Yeah. Once or twice with some friends in college."

"And they were all willing participants?" He looked skeptical.

"Yes."

"Why?"

"Because it's fun. And because it doesn't involve getting drunk."

Colton chuckled. "See, that's where we're different because I would have to be completely slammed to ever agree to hop through a fountain."

"You don't actually hop. You just splash each other and get wet. You *have fun*."

His head shook again. "I can't believe you ever convinced other people to do that with you. Are you sure they didn't sneak a few drinks beforehand?"

"Yes, I'm sure," said Sam. "That was the whole point of our Virgin Adventures."

"Whoa. What did you just say?"

Sam rested her elbow on a rack and sighed. "My mom always joked that if I ever started drinking, it would be the equivalent of a manic person taking Prozac. That was her way of warning me away from alcohol, which she didn't really need to do because I've seen too many friends get drunk and do stupid things to ever want to go there. But when I got to college, it seemed like the thing to do was hang out at bars or dance clubs. Since I didn't want to sit home alone every weekend, it was either become the designated driver or come up with something else.

"I called them Virgin Adventures, and we'd do things like scavenger hunts, skateboard races, or watch movies like *Jaws* in someone's swimming pool. At first, it was just a few of us, but then word got out and more people started joining us. By the end of my first year, we usually had at least fifty people show."

Colton looked impressed. "And you came up with all those ideas?"

"Most of the time. I found a lot online, and every now and then, someone else would have a different idea, so we'd give it a try. Which is a good point to make." She tapped him on the chest with her finger. "We *always* gave every idea, no matter how dumb it sounded, a try. And most of the time, it turned out pretty fun."

Colton slung an arm around her back and guided her toward the front door. "What about a compromise?"

"I'm listening."

"I was thinking I could take you through one of those really cool car washes instead. It'll sort of be like fountain hopping with an umbrella."

Sam had to smile at that. Although his compromising skills needed a little work, in his defense, she'd sprung this whole shopping/fountain thing on him with no warning. Maybe if she'd asked his opinion from the get-go, they could have come up with a real compromise.

True to his word, Colton took her through a long and interesting car wash that felt more like a ride at an amusement park. High powered rotating jets blasted the truck, creating thunderish sounds in the cab. Then large, brightly-colored brushes spun around the truck in various shapes and patterns, beating away every speck of dirt. More jets were followed by powerful dryers that scattered thousands of tiny droplets from the windows. They finished the ride by going through a long wall of mirrors that showcased the shiny clean truck. Pretty impressive.

Sam had been raised as a do-it-yourself girl and had never been through a car wash of quite this caliber.

Afterwards, Colton drove to her favorite café for takeout and they ended up at a large park.

"I was thinking we could put those towels to good use and have a picnic right there." He pointed to a shady spot on the grass, next to a large, circular fountain that sprouted a lovely waterfall. "That's as close as you're going to get me to fountain hopping, I'm afraid."

It wasn't exactly what she'd envisioned for the night, but the date had involved water, towels, and a fountain and they hadn't gone anywhere near a burger joint. Colton had at least *tried* to compromise, she had to give him that.

She leaned over and gave him a kiss on the cheek. "I love picnics."

"I know, right? We get to eat great food, hang out on two towels under that big tree over there, and stay warm and dry and adult."

Sam laughed. "Adulthood is overrated."

"Normally, I'd agree with you."

"But not today?"

"Not today."

"What about tomorrow?"

A smile spread across his face. "Is this how it's going to be from here on out?"

She scooted closer and rested her head against his shoulder. "I just want to make each day from now until the end of summer one to remember."

She felt his shoulder stiffen and the humor left his voice. "What about after this summer?" he said quietly.

The question was so loaded and weighted down that Sam found it hard to pick up. She lifted her head and gazed at him, not liking the clouds she saw in his eyes. She put her hand on his and threaded her fingers in between. "I think every day should be worth remembering. Don't you?"

"Yes." He lifted her fingers and kissed them, though lines of worry were etched in his forehead.

They left the conversation behind, spread out the towels to make a large square, and plopped down to enjoy dinner. The sky was clear, the temperature a tad on the warm side, and the park abuzz with people. Arm in arm, an elderly couple strolled by, not speaking, just enjoying the ambiance. A small group of kids played tag while parents chatted at a nearby picnic table. Other kids played on a playground not far away, and a father threw a football back and forth with his son.

Sam breathed in the fresh, summer air and silently

applauded all the people who'd ventured outside their house to experience life. Because of them, the park pulsated with a strong and positive energy.

"How about we flip the town tomorrow night?" she said.

He paused with his sandwich part way into his mouth then took a deliberate bite, chewing slowly. "I know you don't mean what it sounds like you mean, but I can't come up with anything else it could mean, so . . . you're going to have to explain."

"It'll be fun. We'll drive to the center of town and flip a coin. Heads, we go right. Tails, left. If there's something to do at the next intersection, that's what we do. If not, we keep flipping and driving until we find something else. The last time I did it with a group of people, we ended up singing karaoke, bowling, and eating Indian food. What do you say?"

"What if we toss heads all night and end up driving in circles?"

"Then we potentially sing lots of songs, knock over lots of pins, or eat lots of food."

"Sounds . . . interesting." From the look on his face, "interesting" meant "totally lame."

"Will you at least try it? Please? For me?"

Colton lay down on his back and folded his arms behind his head. "Fine. But if we end up at a karaoke place, I refuse to sing."

"Not even if it's a Garth Brooks song? I thought you were a cowboy."

"Not all cowboys sing."

"What about 'Red Solo Cup'? There's no singing involved in that song. You could totally pull it off."

"There's no brains involved either." He quirked an eyebrow. "Still think I can pull it off?"

She cocked her head to the side as though mulling it over, and he immediately poked her lightly in the ribs. It tickled, and she squirmed away.

His lips lifted into a smile. "Are you ticklish?"

"No."

He executed an effortless sit-up and towered over her, trapping her shoulders between his hands. "I think you are."

"If you tickle me, I'll scream. Loudly. As in, the-police-will-come-running-with-taser-guns loudly. I really, *really* hate being tickled."

He leaned in closer and dropped his voice. "And I really, really hate karaoke. So . . . compromise number two for tonight: If you don't give me any guff about never singing in front of a crowd, I won't tickle you."

His close proximity made her stomach twist and turn. Unable to resist, she pushed the hat off his head and dragged her fingers through his short, thick hair. "Will you at least swing dance or two-step with me while someone else sings?"

"You might talk me into that."

"Then it's a date."

"Yes, ma'am."

Sam's fingers stilled at the nape of his neck, and she lifted an eyebrow. "Ma'am?"

"Would you rather I call you muffin?"

"No."

"Pumpkin?"

"Not on your life."

"Darlin'?" His head inched closer with every attempted endearment, and Sam felt the warmth of his breath on her cheek and saw each line and contour of his face. Dang, he was handsome.

"What about just plain old ordinary Samantha?" she said.

"Because there's nothing plain or ordinary about you, Samantha."

One short sentence, nine simple words, and the world shifted. Sam suddenly found it hard to breathe. Her pounding heart thudded in her ears, and all the background noises of water, squeals, and chirping birds faded away as

Colton closed the distance between them. Slowly and methodically, she kissed him, feeling each sensation, each nerve, each shiver of delight. Her hands palmed his freshly shaved face, following the movements of his jaw. Everything about him felt so right, so strong, so good. He was someone she needed to throw her arms around, hold on tight, and never let go.

New York was definitely negotiable. Colton was not.

The pressure of his lips eased off hers, and he dropped his forehead to hers. His chest rose and fell in cadence with hers, and ever so slowly the outside world began to fade back in. Water gurgled and splashed, birds chirped and sang, kids giggled and squealed, and Colton's voice sounded still and quiet.

"I'm falling in love with you." He didn't preface the words with "I think" or "I'm pretty sure." He stated them with calm conviction.

Her eyes flew open and her breath caught in her throat. Colton looked down at her, his gaze intense. The air around them seemed to spark and snap as though it had just been charged with electricity, and the light behind his head became blinding. A delicious warmth gushed over her like a tidal wave, making her feel like she'd been lifted off the ground and carried away.

This is what magic feels like, Sam thought.

"I'm falling too."

Eighteen

COLTON QUICKLY DISCOVERED that when Samantha said she wanted to make every day count, what she really meant was every second of every minute of every hour of every day. Over the next few weeks, they flipped the town, rented Segways and drove them through the streets of Colorado Springs, went paintballing, and had a moonlight picnic. They rode horses and four-wheelers and even caught a few spectacular sunrises from the small rise above The Shack. Then one morning, she hauled him up the mountain to a place with rock climbing, zip-lining, and ropes courses, and he quickly hauled her back down—at least part way—to some caves. There, he introduced her to a sport that kept them on solid ground—spelunking.

Together, they created memory after memory after memory. Time skittered past like a lizard in the desert, and as the end of July drew near, a nagging thought intruded on all the fun.

Samantha wouldn't care so much about making every second count if she was planning to stay.

Colton was becoming an expert at shoving it aside, but, like a determined fly, it didn't stay gone for long.

On the evening of Kajsa's first barrel race, the McCoys, Mackies, Granthams, and Kinseys all piled into the stands on the south side of the rodeo grounds. When it came time for Kajsa's race, they cheered wildly as she tore through the course, her dark ponytail and pinned-on number flapping in the air behind her. She rode with style and confidence—a natural. But as she circled the last barrel, she cut in too tight and knocked it over. Afterwards, it took a gallon of mint chocolate chip ice cream and Colton's promise to take her with him to the Mustang Makeover Contest to cheer her up.

"Mind if I tag along too?" Samantha had asked.

"Of course not," said Colton, not sure what to think. Her job started in August, and the competition took place in September. Was she planning to fly back for it, or (dare he hope?) still be around? The subject of Samantha's job never really made it into their conversations. Whenever Colton hinted at it, she quickly changed the subject, which wasn't a good sign. Samantha would have told him if she'd turned down the job, which meant she hadn't, which meant . . . what?

After a particularly sleepless night, Colton rose before the sun and saddled Maverick. Riding always cleansed his mind, and today he needed it. As the sun crested the top of the horizon, he galloped across the fields, taking Maverick high into the hills. At a small lookout, Colton pulled him to a stop. Below them, the valley looked unreal, like a tiny model of Colorado Springs you'd find in a visitor's center. It was a view that normally stole his breath, but today, he didn't see anything.

What will I do if Samantha decides to leave?

A feeling of dread settled in his gut, and Colton pulled Maverick around, spurring him higher into the hills. They zigzagged through trees, leapt over small streams, and continued to climb until Maverick's coat glistened with sweat and his breathing became ragged. Still, the dread gnawed. It didn't matter how far he rode, how fresh the air was, or how warm the sun became, he and Maverick couldn't outrun it.

Giving up, Colton finally turned his beloved horse around and rode back down. As he loped up the lane leading to the barn, all was quiet on the ranch. His father and brothers had already left to collect the sheep and broncs for the family rodeo tonight, and his mother was probably at the store. Samantha had given herself several food assignments and wouldn't be coming until later, with her family.

From across the field a giggle sounded, followed by Kajsa's voice. She was talking to Maj. When did she get here?

Colton squinted through the sunlight and saw Kajsa standing—*standing!*—on Maj's bare back with her arms stretched out to the side while the horse stood ramrod still. Her trim body trembled and swayed as she adjusted to stay balanced, and after a moment, she crouched down and straddled the horse, taking a fistful of dark hair in her small hands.

"Let's go, Your Majesty!" she yelled. Off they went, galloping across the field with no saddle or bridle, only one hundred percent trust between an eleven-year-old girl and a one-thousand pound animal that only two months ago had been wild.

Colton had always known that Kajsa had a knack with horses, but he'd attributed it to her lack of fear and youthful, sometimes naïve, trust in the animals. But he'd underestimated her big-time. She had a gift that few had— one that Colton, his father, and his brothers didn't. Self-proclaimed "horse whisperers" were people most ranchers took about as seriously as fortune tellers. They'd been the butt of more than a few jokes over the years. But as Kajsa leaned forward over Maj with her hat low on her forehead, skimming the field the way an eagle might skim the water, in a graceful, fluid way, Colton became a believer.

A thick sensation ran through his veins, and for the first

time all morning, Colton felt peace. Kajsa had just proved that anything was possible, even the impossible.

He swung down from Maverick and took his time caring for his horse. He brushed him down, dug dirt from his hooves, and fed him some oats. Then he released the horse into the field and took a seat on the fence while he waited for Kajsa to return. When she did, her face was flushed and radiant.

Until she spotted Colton.

Immediately, she slid off Maj's back and shoved her hands into her back pockets. Maj jogged away like a coward, leaving her young rider to face Colton alone.

"I, um . . ." Her left boot kicked at the soft earth.

"You, um, what?" Colton wasn't about to make it easy on her.

Her eyes flashed to his before dropping back to the ground. Finally, she shrugged. "Nobody was in the house when Cassie dropped me off, so . . ."

"So you decided to take a barebacked ride on a wild animal?"

"She's not wild." A pause. "And I couldn't get the saddle on her."

"I see," said Colton. "What other choice did you have, right?"

"Um . . ." In her mind, she probably agreed but knew better than to admit it out loud. Kajsa had taken a ride without permission on a horse she'd only been allowed to ride inside an enclosed corral. Yeah, she was way too smart to fall into that trap.

"I'm sorry?" The apology came in the form of a question, as though she wasn't sure if it was the right thing to say.

Colton nearly laughed, knowing she wasn't the least bit sorry. He jumped off the fence and walked toward her, stopping about one foot away. "Tell you what, Kajsa. After careful consideration, I've made a decision this morning.

You're not going to be my training assistant any longer."

Her eyes widened, her jaw dropped slightly, and a mixture of fear, despair, and maybe even some anger flashed in her eyes. "I told you I'm sorry. I really am!"

She meant it this time, and Colton nearly laughed again. He placed his hands on her shoulders and looked into large blue eyes that shined with unshed tears. "From here on out, you're going to be the trainer, and I'm going to be the assistant. At the competition, my name will be listed as the official trainer, but it's you who is going to show those judges what Maj can do."

She blinked once, twice, then joy replaced the despair. "Really?"

He nodded. "You have a gift, Kajsa, and it's high time we started utilizing it. I'm the one who should be sorry for not really seeing you until now."

Kajsa threw her arms around his waist and hugged him fiercely. And then she was gone, running back through the fields, undoubtedly excited to share the good news with Your Majesty. It wasn't her sister, her father, or her new step-mom she wanted to tell first. It was the horse.

His phone buzzed in his pocket with a text, and Colton pulled it out, seeing a message from Samantha.

Thinking of you was all it said.

Colton smiled and slipped the phone back into his pocket before heading toward the barn. For a morning that had begun on a sour note, the day suddenly seemed full of hope and promise.

Nineteen

SAM SLAMMED HER shoulder into Colton's wooden front door again, and again, and again before it finally flew open. Then she lunged for the knob to keep the door from hitting the wall behind it. Colton needed to trim that down. It made it really difficult to sneak into his shack when everyone at the main house had probably heard the loud bang.

She'd come a little late to the barbeque on purpose, wanting to make sure that The Shack was empty so she could come and go undetected. The foil-wrapped wooden sign had been sitting in her top dresser drawer for too long while Sam waited for the perfect opportunity to give it to him. But that time never came. And since Colton's birthday was still five months away, it was either wait until then or give it to him now.

Sam wasn't nearly as patient as Colton.

She crept down the hall and knocked softly on his bedroom door. When no one answered, she pushed it open without a squeal. At least he'd oiled the hinges, she thought as she padded lightly across the floor. The bed was unmade and some jeans and a few shirts were thrown across the footboard. Other than that, it was pretty clean. Sam tugged the dark gray comforter back in place, plumped his two mismatched pillows, and made the bed look as decent as she could. Then she set the present down in the middle.

As she stepped back to make sure everything looked okay, she noticed a small framed picture on his nightstand. The night of their first date—the rodeo—Colton had put his arm around her and pulled her close for a selfie shot. He'd texted her a copy, and she'd made it the background image on her phone, but she hadn't gone so far as to print and frame it. But Colton had, and the sight of it made her insides feel all bubbly and fizzy, like sparkling apple cider.

Behind her, the floorboards squeaked, and Colton's voice called out, "Sam? Are you here?"

She quickly set the frame down, but it fell over. Before she could right it, his voice came again. "There you are."

Leaving it lying on his nightstand, she stood and turned around, feeling like an intruder. He rested his shoulder against the door jamb and folded his arms, cocking his head at her. "Breaking and entering?"

She clasped her fingers together and moved to block his view of the present. He'd never seen any of her designs, and she'd rather not be around when he saw this one. If he didn't like it, she'd be crushed.

"If anything's broken, it's my shoulder. When are you going to fix that door once and for all?"

"When I get around to it." His brow lifted. "What's going on?"

"Oh, I was just . . ." What now? Sam hadn't planned on getting caught. "Um . . . looking for an earring that I'm pretty sure I lost here." It sounded even lamer out loud.

"In my room?"

"Well, I couldn't find it in your great room, so, you know, I thought you might have, uh . . . stepped on it with a muddy boot and tracked it in here. I mean, stranger things have happened, right?" Wow, she was really bad at this.

Colton's lips twitched.

"You know what?" she blurted. "We should go." She grabbed his hand, trying to pull him down the hall, but he hooked an arm around her waist and held her close. "You could have just said you were leaving me a gift and didn't want me to open it until after you were gone."

Of course he'd seen it. The shiny foil reflected the light like a sparkly diamond. Sam should have wrapped it in gray camouflage. "Okay, fine. I am leaving you a gift and really, really, *really* don't want you to open it until after I'm gone."

"Gone where?" Although his eyes glinted with humor, there was an underlying hint of serious.

"Home. Tonight. After the rodeo."

He nodded and released her waist, stepping toward the bed. "What if I don't want to wait?"

"You're the most patient person I know. Of course you can wait."

Colton picked up the present and smoothed a hand over the package. "I didn't say I *couldn't* wait. I said I didn't want to. What is it?"

"Nothing really. Just a belated thanks-for-the-riding-lessons present." She wrung her hands, feeling nervous and vulnerable. "What are you doing here, anyway? Shouldn't you be helping your parents with the barbeque?"

"Everything's all ready. I just came back to change real quick. It's hot out there."

"Oh, okay. Well, I'll leave you to it then and see you over there." She took a step toward the door, but he grabbed her arm to keep her in the room. "Not so fast. I suddenly find myself really curious about this present."

"Curiosity kills cats."

"But not humans." He smiled and sat down, pulling her on to his lap.

"Are you really going to open that in front of me?"

"I really am."

"You're mean."

His arms wound around her waist, and he pulled her against him. Then he slid off the bow and tore open the foil and tissue paper.

"What's this?" He ran his fingers across the top the way a blind person might do, touching all the grooves and edges.

"A sign. To hang next to your front door." When he didn't say anything, she added, "But only if you like it."

"I love it." Colton held it closer to his face, inspecting the details. "Did you make this?" His voice held a note of reverence, and Sam nearly sighed in relief. Oh good. He liked it.

"I only designed it. A professional sign company lasered the image into the wood."

"But you drew this?" He pointed to the simple graphic of a cabin surrounded by a few trees.

She nodded. "On the computer. I manipulated the font a little to make it fit around the image right there and there." She shrugged. "It's what I do."

"I know. I just . . ." A pause. "Wow, you're really good. I mean *really* good. Thank you. It's awesome."

Sam twisted on his lap so she could see him better. Under the rim of his hat, his eyes looked inky and mysterious. She wanted to run her fingers along the defined contours of his arms, shoulders, chest, and neck and feel the scruff from his five o'clock shadow. She wanted to feel his breath on her neck and his hands in her hair. But mostly, she wanted him to understand how conflicted she felt about the job and him.

"I *am* good," she said quietly, her eyes pleading with his. "The job in New York isn't just any job. It's *the* job. Brecken Design is internationally ranked at number four, and out of hundreds of applicants, I'm the one they chose. I have an opportunity to learn from the best of the best and be involved with the kind of projects most designers only dream about." She hesitated. "It's the kind of opportunity that doesn't exist in Colorado Springs or even Denver."

The edges of his eyes crinkled, and it looked like it took effort for him to swallow. "So what you're saying is that you're going."

Sam placed her hands on the sides of his face and forced him to look at her. "I'm saying I'm greedy. I want both you and the job."

"You want me to move to New York?"

"No. I would never ask you to do that. I know your life is here." She bit down on her lower lip for a moment before continuing. "But I want to ask you something else."

"What?"

"I love you," she said. "More than anything, I want to spend the rest of my life with you. But if I turn down this job, I'll always wonder what I could have done, what I could have learned. So I'm going to ask you something I have no right to ask. To wait. Give me two years, and I'll be back. Just two years."

Colton didn't say anything. He just watched her with dark, cloudy, mysterious eyes. Unreadable eyes. What was he thinking?

"I'll come home as often as I can, and you can fly out to see me. We can—"

"I don't fly," he interrupted.

"What?"

"I. Don't. Fly. I've never once set foot on an airplane."

Sam blinked, trying to understand what he was saying. "There's a first time for everything," she said, her voice small.

He sighed and slid her to the side, off his lap. Then he stood and turned around, shoving his hands into his pockets. "You don't understand. I have a crippling fear of heights. Any time I get higher than ten feet off the ground, the world starts spinning and I can't catch my breath. It's so bad, I can't climb a ladder to fix a broken shingle on the roof."

Sam stood slowly. "So that's why you refused to go ziplining or rock climbing."

"Yes."

"But airplanes are different," she tried. "I mean, you're inside them, and when you're up in the air it feels like you're just in a tall tower, looking down."

He shook his head. "I can't do tall towers either."

"Then you can shut the windows and sit in an aisle seat."

He was still shaking his head, and so many of her hopes begin to crumble. She'd envisioned them walking together through Central Park, taking in some Broadway shows, and going to see touristy things like the Statue of Liberty or the Empire State Building. And what about traveling the world at some point? There were so many places Sam wanted to see; so many cultures she wanted to experience. If she married Colton, would she be destined to do it all without him? Or give up those dreams altogether?

All of their little compromises and differences suddenly felt so much bigger. Colton was like a sturdy evergreen, strong and tall, patient and unwavering and perfectly content to root deeply in the soil. Sam, on the other hand, wanted to be the wind that blew through the trees, free to soar high or skim low, free to touch, taste, and feel all she could. But she didn't want to do it alone. She wanted Colton along for the ride.

"Okay," she breathed, feeling like her chest had been squeezed in a vice. "I'll visit you then."

"Or," he said, looking at her with pain-filled eyes. "You can move on with your life, and I'll move on with mine. If you do come back in two years, we can see what happens then."

If she'd thought her hopes had been crushed before, now they'd been pulverized. He wasn't even willing to try to compromise this time. From the sounds of it, he didn't even want to stay in touch.

A part of her heart cracked open, and unwanted tears began to grow at the corners of her eyes. Maddening, frustrating tears. *Go away!* she wanted to shout. *I'm stronger than this. I can take it. I CAN.* But instead of drying up, more and more tears came. So many that they leaked from her eyes and traveled down her cheeks.

Angrily, she swiped them away and glared at the person who'd caused them. "Sometimes, I really hate that you can be such a stick-in-the-mud."

Then she pushed past him and ran out the door, back to her car. A quick U-turn later, and she sped down the lane, away from Colton, away from the ranch, and away from all the people who were completely oblivious that her heart had just broken in two.

Colton sank down on his bed and picked up the sign, running his fingers across the top with slow and deliberate movements, tracing each letter and image. Samantha was right. She *was* good. And if a highly-ranked company like that Brecken whatever had chosen her out of hundreds, she was even better than good.

Before now, Colton hadn't realized what New York truly meant. He'd thought it was a design job like any other—a job she could find in Denver or Colorado Springs at the local Kinkos or Color Me Mine. Now he understood, and the knowledge slammed into him like the ground after he'd been bucked off a horse.

There was no keeping her here, no hoping she'd choose him instead of a job. Samantha *had* to leave. She'd regret it if she didn't, and Colton—well, he'd never be able to live with himself if she stayed because of him. That scenario had disaster written all over it.

But the scenario in which she left and Colton stayed didn't sound much better. This was a solid case of life sucked.

What could he do, though? Samantha had been right

when she'd said his life was here. It was. Colton was tied to the ranch like a horse tethered to a post. Animals needed to be watered and fed every day. Stalls needed to be cleaned. Taxes needed to be paid. Riding lessons needed to be taught. And horses needed to be looked after and trained.

His family had never taken a vacation together because they couldn't. Not even for a day. They were a tight-knit group—not because they played together but because they *worked* together. When Colton had left with Will to round up wild mustangs for a week, his family had stepped in to pick up the slack, just like they'd pitched in to help out with some of his share of the work this summer because of Maj. And Colton did the same for them when needed.

But those were all short-term scenarios. A week here, a week there. A few hours here, a few hours there. Handing over his share of the responsibilities for an entire two years was out of the question, which meant he had to stay.

And Samantha had to go.

Until this moment, Colton's ties to the ranch had never felt confining.

Twenty

BY THE TIME Sam had pulled herself together enough to go to the barbeque it was well underway. Cassie's entire side of the family had come, along with some of the McCoy's friends and neighbors. People were everywhere, chatting, eating, and laughing as though life was grand. It felt like a slap in the face.

After forcing herself to greet everyone, Sam settled down with Georgia on her lap. But her stomach began rumbling loudly, and Emma snatched Georgia back and shooed Sam toward the buffet table.

"Eat," she said. "You're too thin as it is."

As Sam walked to the food table, her eyes scanned the crowd, finally landing on a group of people clustered near the grill. Colton stood next to a beautiful girl with long brown hair and a skirt that was far too flirty and cute. Sam hated her instantly. Colton chuckled at something she said, as though all was fine and dandy with the world.

Well, it wasn't. Sam wanted to walk straight over to him and say, "Wipe that smile off your face right now. You're not allowed to be happy and pretend like nothing is wrong when everything's wrong."

As if sensing her presence, the cute girl glanced up and elbowed Colton, nodding in Sam's direction. Colton followed her gaze, and for a moment their eyes met. But Sam quickly looked away and pasted a matching smile on her own face. If Colton could act unaffected, then so could she. If he could put on a happy face and find someone to flirt with—well, so could she. Only in her case, she'd find a handsome guy who liked to sing karaoke and hop through fountains and travel the world.

Her gaze landed on a man sitting across from Adi and Kajsa and laughing at something Adi had said.

Sam walked to the buffet table, grabbed a roll, a spoonful of fruit salad, and some chips and took a seat next to the good-looking cowboy.

"Hey, Adi and Kajsa."

"You're late," said Kajsa.

"Guilty."

The rebound cowboy glanced her way for a moment. "Well, ladies," he said, speaking to Adi and Kajsa. "Are you going to introduce me or not?"

Sam didn't bother waiting. She held out her hand. "I'm Sam Kinsey, their almost-sister. And you are?"

He tipped the brim of his black cowboy hat. "Will. Will Jeppson. My family's ranch is on the other side of that mountain."

Sam lifted a chip to her mouth and tapped the edge against her lower lip. "Tell me something, Will. How do you feel about flying?"

And so it went the rest of the night. Sam flirted with Will briefly (until he asked her if she was Colton's "Sam"), and then she moved on to someone else. Meanwhile, the annoyingly cute brunette continued to hang around Colton, batting her too-long-to-be real lashes at him and touching him every chance she got. Eventually, Sam got fed up with all the pretending and wandered back to the buffet, trying hard to keep her mood elevated, her smile intact, and her threatening tears at bay.

Tonight was a night she'd looked forward to all summer. Kajsa would be riding Whisper in a barrel race, Dusty would be riding a bronc, and Spence was all dressed up in baggy jeans, suspenders, and a zany shirt with colorful, neon stripes going every which way. Sam wanted to get caught up in it all, push the annoying cute-girl aside, and take her rightful spot next to Colton.

If only a thunderstorm would roll in, let loose a deluge, and put an end to this miserable night.

"Hey, you." Her mother appeared at her side and picked up a baby carrot. "I noticed you came a little late to the party. You're never late to parties."

"Something came up."

"What?"

"Nothing."

"You just said it was something."

"It *was* something. Now it's nothing." Sam shoved another chip in her mouth, knowing that if her mother continued she'd likely burst into tears again.

Her mother bit off some of the carrot and chewed slowly. Even though Sam refused to look up, she could feel her mother's perceptive gaze watching her, seeing far more than Sam wanted her to see.

Finally, her mother's arm came around her, and she placed a soft kiss on Sam's temple. "We'll talk later, okay?"

"Okay."

"In the meantime," said her mother with a bright, spunky tone, "exciting news about Kajsa, huh?" Sam's expression must have shown her confusion, because her mother continued, "Apparently Colton has made her head trainer of Maj."

"What?" Sam's head snapped up. "When did that happen?"

"Sometime this morning, I think. You know Kajsa. When she's really excited, not much of what she says makes sense."

Sam nodded, thinking of the occasions she'd had to plant both palms on Kajsa's shoulders, give them a slight shake and say, "Kajsa, take five deep breaths *then* tell me what's gotten you all discombobbled."

"I had no idea," said Sam, not liking the fact that she'd gone from being in the loop to out of it in a matter of hours. Stupid New York job. Stupid stick-in-the-mud Colton. And stupid bright blue skies with not a cloud in sight. Where was that deluge when she needed it?

Colton's voice sounded over the loudspeakers. "Who's ready to get this party started?" His tone had taken on a southern, twangy quality that Sam had always found adorable. Now it grated.

Cheers sounded from all around—from everyone but Sam. If he would have said, "Who's ready to call it quits and go home?" she would have hollered her head off.

The rodeo began. Five men rode broncs, three women competed in the barrel races (Kajsa performed perfectly this time), four men did some sheep roping, and nineteen kids lined up to climb on the back of a sheep and hang on for dear life. Over and over again. They'd fall off the sheep and jump right back in line to do it again. Between every ride and event, Spence would jog out center field and act like an idiot.

Gradually, Sam felt her sour mood begin to sweeten. She laughed when Dusty got bucked right off, cheered loudly for Kajsa, chuckled at all the failed attempts at roping a sheep, and giggled as child after child bounced along on the back of a sheep then toppled to the ground. So adorable.

By the time the rodeo ended, she'd almost forgotten that she and Colton were on the outs. Almost. With his voice blaring in her ears the entire night, giving humorous remarks about each and every ride, she couldn't forget completely.

"Before everyone finishes off the last of my mother's

amazing mint brownies," Colton's voice came again, "I have a demonstration I'd like ya'll to see. A finale. Kajsa, would you come up here for a second?"

Her face flushed with embarrassment and pleasure, Kajsa made her way to the front of the crowd. Colton draped an arm around her shoulders. "This morning I was able to witness a sight that blew my socks off, and it's something I'd like to share with the rest of you.

"As many of you know, I've been training a horse for the Wild Mustang Makeover contest in Fort Worth, Texas, this September. At the beginning of June, I showed up with a horse as wild as they come, wondering what in the heck I'd gotten myself into."

Laughter and murmuring followed, and Colton waited for it to die down before continuing. "Not only did Kajsa give the horse its name of Your Majesty, but she understood the wild mustang's personality and needs in a way that an average dope like me couldn't. About two months ago, Maj rode up to this ranch kicking and screaming, determined not to let anyone near her, and now—well, watch and see."

He nodded at Kajsa, and Sam squeezed through the crowd of people wanting a clear view. As she neared the front, she looked up to find Colton's eyes on her. The intensity in them stole her breath away and caused her heart to burn and ache and hope, all at the same time. Him going his way and her going hers was not okay and never would be okay. They had to get through this.

A loud whistle pierced the air, and Sam followed the sound to where Kajsa stood in the open field with her fingers in her mouth. In the other hand, she held a carrot. Seconds later, Maj burst through a grove of trees, running toward Kajsa and stopping directly in front of her. Kajsa fed the mustang the carrot, spoke a few words in her ear, then picked up an empty bucket and flipped it over beside Maj. The horse stood amazingly still as Kajsa hopped on the bucket, grabbed a fist of her mane, and swung up on the horse's back. Using only her voice and a hand on Maj's neck, Kajsa guided the mustang through a small obstacle course, walking across a bridge, around a barrel, and over a pile of logs. Then she loped the perimeter of the larger corral before bringing Maj to a stop near the fence. Ever so slowly, she raised her body into a crouch. Then, with her arms outstretched, she stood.

Tears stung Sam's eyes as she watched. Hours spent making mud pies, watching horse movies, reading horse books, shopping for cowgirl hats and boots had all culminated into this one perfect moment, when an adorable little tomboy became a beautiful young woman. Her sister.

Kajsa crouched back down and slid off the horse. Whistles and whoops and hollers sounded in the darkening sky, but Kajsa seemed oblivious to it all. She was too busy hugging Maj.

More than anything, Sam wanted to talk to Colton, but he was already surrounded by a group of people—the annoying-cute girl being one of them. She took a step back to make room for the others.

A balding man Sam thought was Colton's uncle raised his voice. "Colt, do you think you have a shot at actually winning the competition?"

"I don't know," said Colton in his humble way. "Kajsa and I have watched a few documentaries about other trainers and horses, and what some of those trainers can do with those animals is incredible. Standing on the back of the horse might be small change in comparison."

"Well, here's hoping you at least place. I'd hate to see you come home with nothing after all your hard work."

"What do you mean nothin'?'" boomed Colton's father. "Not only will Maj be placed in a good home, but Kajsa has proven that she's got some serious talent. I wouldn't call that nothin'."

"Oh, I wasn't saying—"

"What do you mean Maj will be placed in a good

home?" interrupted Kajsa's youthful, but strong voice. She'd climbed the fence next to Colton and perched her small body on top.

"The person who bids the highest on Maj will take her home," said Colton. He craned his head to look at her. "But you already know that, right?" The question didn't sound so sure—more like a plea. *Please tell me you already know that,* thought Sam.

"You're going to sell Your Majesty?"

Oh no. She had no idea. Sam's heart sank to her toes.

The crowd around Colton began to disperse, as though people realized an uncomfortable conversation was about to take place. But Sam stayed put, inwardly pleading with Colton to say or do something to keep Kajsa's heart and spirit from breaking.

Colton stepped on the bottom rail of fence, eye level with Kajsa, and placed his hand on her knee. "I can't sell a horse I don't own, Kaj. The government owns her. I just agreed to train her with the hope that she'll get placed in a good home."

In all the years she'd known Kajsa, Sam could count on one hand the number of times she'd seen her cry. It didn't happen often because she was tough—tougher than any other girl her age. But there, on that fence, surrounded by all these people, Kajsa's beautiful blue eyes glistened with tears.

"Can we buy her?" she whispered, a final hope hanging in the air like a thin, breakable thread. *Don't break it. Please, don't break it,* her eyes pled.

Colton pulled her off the fence and into his arms, hugging her tight. "I wish we could, Kaj. I really do. But if Maj performs well, people are going to bid thousands of dollars for her, and we can't afford to compete with that."

Kajsa's body began to shake with silent tears. After a moment, she wriggled her way out of Colton's embrace, scrambled over the fence, and ran toward Maj in the field. Every instinct in Sam pushed her to follow, but Cassie and

Noah had overheard as well, and they were already in pursuit.

Colton's stricken gaze met Sam's. "I thought she knew. I honestly thought she knew. But how could she when I never took the time to explain it to her?" He closed his eyes and shook his head.

Sam wanted to touch him, comfort him, tell him everything would be okay, but there was still too much distance between them for that. She said nothing.

It was Colton's father who spoke up. "Kajsa is the toughest girl I know," he said. "She'll be just fine. If she's going to be a real horse trainer some day, she needs to learn that letting horses go is part of the business."

It sounded so harsh and cold, but Sam knew he spoke the truth. Kajsa was learning a hard lesson in the worst way possible—through firsthand experience.

"Sam." Her mother was suddenly at her side, her hand on Sam's elbow.

"Yeah?"

"What do you say we help clean up?"

Sam nodded. Clean up. Of course. She met Colton's gaze one last time before walking away. The rodeo had been the calm between storms. Why couldn't it have lasted a little longer?

Sam couldn't sleep and had too much on her mind to even attempt it. So she took a seat in front of her computer, opened Photoshop, and scrolled through a folder of JPEG images until she found her favorite picture of Kajsa and Maj. Taken right after Kajsa's first ride on Maj, Kajsa had wrapped the reins around the saddle horn and leaned low over Maj's neck, giving the horse an exuberant hug. The look of joy and trust on Kajsa's face was what Sam loved the most—that and the cool camera angle that had captured it all.

Zooming in close on the saddle horn, Sam began to work the magic of Photoshop. Minutes and hours ticked by unnoticed as Sam erased, blended, cloned, painted, and blended some more, removing all signs of the saddle from the image to make it look like Kajsa was riding bareback. She added a photo effect that roughened the edges of the picture and adjusted the colors, fading some and brightening others. When Sam finally pushed her chair back to examine the results from a distance, the picture that had been snapped with a cell phone now looked like a realistic pastel drawing of Kajsa and the wild mustang she'd come to love so much.

The clock on her nightstand glowed with the time of five-thirteen when Sam clicked Save and shut down the computer then crawled into bed. Kajsa wouldn't be ready to see it anytime soon, but someday, when the good memories overshadowed the loss, she would be ready. Sam would hold onto the picture until that day.

Twenty-one

ANOTHER SLEEPLESS NIGHT and early morning ride did nothing for Colton's state of mind. After getting bucked off Maj three consecutive times, he stripped the saddle, released her into the field, and kicked a fence post. A lot of good that did. Not only were none of his problems solved but now his foot throbbed.

His father's proclamation that "She'll be just fine," was bologna. Last night, as Kajsa left with Cassie and Noah, tears still streaming down her face, she'd glared at him. "I'm never coming to the ranch again." She'd sounded so serious, so set, that he worried she'd meant every word.

And then there was Samantha.

Boy howdy, had Colton made a mess of things.

His mother's tired and crippled minivan puttered up the driveway, stopping in front of the house. She got out, took one look at him, and said, "I could use some help with the groceries."

Colton nodded, glad for something to do.

His mother followed him inside. She didn't believe in shooting the breeze. "I just got off the phone with Cassie, and

Kajsa's still pretty upset. Cassie thinks it best to let her stay away until after the competition and auction."

Colton shook his head, hating that it had come to this. "I've been thinking, Mom."

Her expression became wary. "What about?"

"What if we remortgaged part of the ranch—enough to buy back Maj?"

Her eyes softened, and she shook her head. "It's a sweet thought, honey, it really is, but you know we can't do that. We're barely making ends meet as it is. And when your father and I first got married, we made a promise to each other that we would never let it come to that, no matter how tight things got. I'm sorry, but remortgaging the ranch isn't an option."

"What about selling of some of the land that borders Colorado Springs? Developers have been after that section of our property for years now." Colton's stomach clenched at the thought. All seventy-nine acres of the ranch had been in the McCoy family for over one hundred years. Letting some of it go would be like selling part of their souls. But what other options were there?

"Do you really think that's a good idea?"

"No."

"Neither do I."

Colton rifled through the bags, pulling out boxes and cans and shoving them into the pantry. "If I'd have explained everything to Kajsa in the beginning, this wouldn't have happened. It's my fault she got so attached; my fault she thought the horse was ours to keep."

His mother touched his arm. "Kajsa would have become attached regardless. You know that."

"Which is exactly the point," he said. "She and Maj share a special connection—a rare connection. I can't stand by and watch it break. They need each other."

"Need?" His mother arched an eyebrow with that look

that made him feel like she could see inside his soul. "Are you sure we're still talking about Maj and Kajsa?"

"Who else would we be talking about?"

"You and Sam."

Colton's body stiffened. She hadn't meant to pour salt on an open wound; she probably thought she was offering him a Band Aid. A good talk and everything would be okay. But it wouldn't. There was no solution that would close the gap between Colorado and New York. Words, hugs, money—they wouldn't cut it. And Colton didn't want to think about it anymore.

Kajsa and Maj, on the other hand, he could do something about.

"This has nothing to do with me and Samantha," his said. "We're talking about Kajsa and Maj and that's it."

"You sure?"

"Positive."

"If you say so." She pulled open the fridge to put away some produce. "Tell you what. If you can think of another way to raise several thousand dollars to buy a wild mustang for an eleven-year-old girl, I will do whatever I can to help."

When she put it that way, it sounded ridiculous and unreasonable. Maybe his father was right. Maybe this was a lesson Kajsa would need to learn sooner or later, and now was as good a time as any. But Colton couldn't leave it alone. There were too many layers; too many people who now suffered because of his lack of communication. He'd see the pain in Kajsa's eyes, in her parents', and in Samantha's. That had hurt the worst. It had been like reliving the aftermath of their earlier conversation all over again.

If there was something he could do to make this right, he was going to do it.

We need to talk.

Sam stared at the words she'd typed into the message app on her phone and frowned, then quickly deleted them.

With a sigh, she tossed the phone on her bed and collapsed beside it. Surely she could come up with something more original to send Colton than that. She was a creative person and "We need to talk" was the most overused phrase in the history of relationships. It was cliché, and she didn't want anything about her relationship with Colton to be cliché.

But she and Colton *did* need to talk. They needed to find a way past this division between them. She couldn't live with it for much longer.

A jingle sounded from her phone—the Colton-specific jingle she'd assigned to his name the day he'd first given her his number. She tensed, afraid she'd conjured up the sound the way a severely dehydrated man could conjure up water.

The jingle came again.

Two texts?

And again.

Three?

Sam grabbed her phone, her fingers shaking as she opened the messages.

38.869969, -104.921504

21:30

Please come.

She tried to get her sleep-deprived mind to make sense of the numbers. Of course, *he'd* come up with something creative, inventive, and non-cliché. Or had he? The numbers meant nothing to her. Maybe his autocorrect feature had glitched and only made it appear like a creative, inventive message.

Or maybe it was some sort of code she had to decipher.

Sam chewed on her lower lip. She was terrible at puzzles and therefore hated them. Where was the key? The explanation? The hint?

For five minutes, she waited for another message. When no more came, she jogged downstairs. "Mom? Dad? Where are you?"

"In here, sweetheart," came her mother's voice.

Sam found her parents in the family room watching a Saturday morning news program. She shoved the phone in front of her mother's face. "Any idea what this means?"

Her mother pushed it back and squinted at the text. "Looks like a math problem to me. But what's with the comma and colon?"

"Let me see." Her father took the phone and read the messages. His brow crinkled for a few moments before clearing. "Oh, I get it."

"What?" Sam and her mother said in unison.

"Try copying and pasting the numbers of the first message into a Google search engine and see what happens." At least her father had been kind enough to give her a hint. That was more than Sam could say for Colton.

Sam did a quick copy and paste job. The top result that came back included a Google map with the caption: *Pike National Forest, 100 Cave of the Winds Rd, West Colorado Springs, CO.*

"They're latitude and longitude coordinates," her father explained. "And the second message is military time. He wants you to meet him tonight at nine-thirty at the location of those coordinates. I'm assuming you know where it is?"

"Yes. Cave of the Winds. He took me spelunking there last week."

"Well, there you go. Apparently you can't get enough of spelunking."

"Or maybe Colton can't get enough of Sam," murmured her mother with a smile.

Sam's heart became light and fluttery. She plunked

down on the sofa and reread the creative, inventive, and non-cliché message. He wanted to see her again. Tonight. At nine-thirty. She couldn't wait.

Twenty-two

THE ROAD TO Cave of the Winds wound back and forth a little more than Sam remembered; the curves a little tighter. Twilight cast a grayed-out hue on everything, and the only things that looked familiar were the dark evergreens set against the backdrop of variegated red and peach rock cliffs. Sam was beginning to worry she'd turned off the highway too soon when the visitor's center had finally appeared. Dark and closed down for the night, the place looked eerie. A few cars remained in the parking lot, but neither of them were Colton's truck, so she circled around and drove down a short hill to the lower, completely vacant parking lot.

What now?

Sam squinted through the dark, finally spotting Colton's truck off to the right, in the middle of an overflow area. Sam parked next to the truck, got out, and peered through the passenger window. Still no Colton.

"In here." A hand waved at her from the bed of his truck.

She found him lying on a navy and plaid blanket with his hat resting next to his head.

"Hey," he said.

She climbed into the truck and sat down beside him. He didn't say anything, only stared up at the nearly black sky, not blinking. An awkward silence settled around them, but Sam didn't know how to un-awkward it, so she pulled her knees to her chest and waited.

Then waited some more.

When he still said nothing, she laid next to him, leaving enough space so only their shoulders touched. "What are you looking at?"

"You mean what am I looking *for*."

"Okay. What are you looking *for*?"

"A shooting star."

She felt all tingly and on edge, her body hyper aware of his. Every inch of her wanted to curl into him, to feel his arms around her, his breath on her neck, his mouth against hers.

"What are you going to wish for?" she asked.

"If I tell you, it won't come true."

Sam knew exactly what *she'd* wish for. She'd had it ready to go for weeks now.

I wish that Brecken Design would move to Colorado Springs.

It could happen, right? Her mom could find the company a sweet deal on some real estate, and the entire team could uproot and come to her. Totally doable. Totally within the realm of possible.

Maybe that was the point of tonight. They'd both wish on a shooting star and let magic figure things out for them. Sounded like a great solution to her.

Unfortunately, no shooting stars appeared.

Finally, Colton rolled to his side and looked at her—really looked at her—as though he wanted to make sure she was listening.

"I'll wait," he said. "For two years, I'll wait. Even longer if I have to."

"You will?" she breathed.

"Yes."

"But—"

"No buts. Period."

It was exactly what she'd wanted to hear only a few days ago. But now it didn't feel like a compromise. It felt like she'd won and he'd lost. Even though the separation would be hard on both of them, his sacrifice was greater, and how was that fair?

Colton tried to smile, but it didn't reach his eyes. He looked . . . sad. He lifted his hand to smooth his knuckles across her cheek. "I'm going to miss you."

Sam caught his hand and tightened her fingers around his. "I need to say something."

"I'm listening."

Sam bit her lip, piecing words together in her mind, trying to find the right fit.

Last night, when I saw you with that girl—

No, that wasn't right.

What if I do take the job and—

Wrong again.

And then they came, flowing out of her mouth like a babbling brook. "I want you to know that you are more important to me than any job or any opportunity, and if you and I are ever in jeopardy over this, I'll quit and catch the next flight back home. *You* are my destination. This job is just a detour."

He nodded and swallowed, looking down at their tangled fingers before clearing his throat. His voice sounded raw with emotion when he said, "I'm okay with that."

"You are? I mean—we are? Okay, I mean. We're going to be okay?" She needed to know this wasn't going to break them. That her leaving really was just a detour. "I have to admit, last night when I saw you flirting with that cute girl in the white skirt—"

"You mean my cousin?"

"She's your cousin?"

He chuckled, and Sam realized how much she'd missed the richness of his laugh. "Yes."

"But she kept touching you."

"She's that way with everyone. She's a hugger and a toucher. I don't think she can help it."

"Oh." Didn't Sam feel sheepish, especially considering she'd tried to "get him back" by flirting with Will and that other guy whose name she couldn't remember.

"Is that why you were trying to flirt with Will and Zeke?"

He made it sound like she was a naïve pre-teen who had no idea how to engage a member of the opposite sex. "I wasn't *trying* to flirt. I *was* flirting."

His chuckle came again. "I wasn't implying that you didn't know how to flirt, only that it probably didn't get you very far."

That was supposed to make her feel better? "I didn't get very far with them because I didn't want it to go far."

"No. You didn't get very far because they both know you're already taken and I would have turned them into mincemeat if they'd so much as given you a second look."

"Oh." Now *that* made her feel good. Warm and sudsy and lusciously-fragrant good. "Am I taken?"

"Yes. Or, at least almost." He lifted his body and rolled closer, hovering over the top of her. Sam fought the urge to grab his shirt and pull him against her. "We need to seal the deal first."

"How do we do that?" she asked.

He drew closer, and his warm and minty breath sent a slew of goose bumps skittering down her spine. "You tell me."

He was making it really hard to think. "Want me to sign something?"

"Nope."

"Handshake?"

"Nuh uh."

"Verbal agreement?"

His lips were brushing her cheek, and she felt them lift into a smile. "Now you're getting closer."

Then his mouth captured hers. An eruption of chills, thrills, and trembles flowed through her body, igniting each nerve. Sam wound her arms around his back, pressing him closer. He tasted like mint, smelled like soap, and felt like heaven. She couldn't get enough.

His lips moved to her neck, and a myriad of sensations rolled across her skin. When his lips found hers again, she felt like she'd been transported to a world where thousands of turquoise butterflies beat their wings against the backdrop of vibrant, double rainbows and gushing waterfalls. New York suddenly felt like a black hole getting in the way of paradise.

I'm not going, she thought. *I can't.*

Gradually, the pressure of his kiss lightened, and he dropped to her side, pulling her against him, his heavy breathing mingling with her hair. Sam burrowed her face into his chest. This was home. Right here. A place she never wanted to leave.

After a few moments of silence, he said, "I have a favor to ask you. It involves Kajsa."

He didn't need to say anything more than that. Any favor he asked was a favor granted. Especially when it came to one of her sisters. "I'm in."

Colton stood back in awe as Samantha became the Energizer Bunny at warp speed. She contacted all of her former college and high school friends and asked if they'd be willing to donate their skills and talents for a good cause, then organized an online service auction. With Adi's help, she created and delivered flyers to all the neighborhoods around her house, rounding up items no longer needed. A week later, they held a massive garage sale and actually made a fair amount of money.

Through it all, Kajsa had no idea the effort being made on her behalf. No one wanted to lift her hopes only to see them crash down if they couldn't raise enough to buy Maj. Auctions were tricky that way. The final price wasn't set until the last bid had been made. But Kajsa began coming to the ranch again, sans her usual enthusiasm. In its place was a solemn sorrow that lingered around her like her own little raincloud.

The only other downside to all the money-making, fund-raising hoopla was that Colton didn't see Samantha nearly as often, and the morning of her departure came way too soon. Samantha had already said her see-you-laters to the McCoys, Mackies, and Granthams. She'd tried to do the same with Colton, attempting to convince him that airport goodbyes were the worst, but he wouldn't hear of it. So on the morning of August twenty-fourth, with a heaviness in his chest and what felt like Kajsa's raincloud hanging overhead, Colton pulled into the driveway behind Samantha's little yellow Bug. How long would it sit there until she came back?

Mrs. Kinsey greeted him at the door with red-rimmed, tear-filled eyes. She threw her arms around Colton, as though it was him leaving and not Sam. "It's because of you she'll be back," she whispered. "Thank you for that."

Her words touched him, and he had to swallow his emotion. Over Mrs. Kinsey's shoulder, Samantha appeared, dragging a large purple suitcase behind her. Looking gorgeous in a pale-yellow, knee-length dress, it took every ounce Colton's willpower to take the large suitcase from her grasp and carry it out to the car instead of back upstairs. Mr. Kinsey followed behind with another, equally large suitcase.

She's leaving. She's really leaving.

Colton had wished so hard that this day would never come, and yet here it was.

"I'll mail the rest of your stuff as soon as I can," promised Mrs. Kinsey, giving her daughter one final hug.

"Thank you," said Samantha, her voice shaky and quiet. "I'll see you in six weeks. Right?"

"Our tickets are already booked."

Samantha hugged her father next. "I'm glad you're coming too."

"As though I'd ever let your mother visit without me. Someone's got to monitor the credit card usage."

Samantha smiled and sniffed and blinked so fast it probably looked as though someone had turned on a strobe light. Then she jumped in the truck, slammed the door behind her, and stared straight ahead.

Colton held out his hand for Mr. Kinsey to take. "Thanks for letting me take her, sir."

Mr. Kinsey shook his hand and clapped Colton on his shoulder. "Drive safe, okay?"

"Will do."

He nodded goodbye to Mrs. Kinsey then jumped in next to Samantha and turned the key, revving the engine. She continued to stare straight ahead, still blinking fast.

Colton clasped her shaky hand in his and held it the entire drive to the Denver airport. When they arrived, he helped her check her luggage, get her boarding pass, and slowly walked with her to security. When he could go no farther, he pulled her into his arms and held on as tight as he could without crushing her. Her body trembled against his and a sob escaped.

She raised tear-filled eyes to his. "Why am I doing this?"

Colton cupped her cheeks with his large hands and swiped the tears from under her eyes. "Because you're

Samantha Kinsey and you can do anything. Why not New York?"

Through her tears, she smiled.

"You're going be the best junior designer they've ever hired, and in six months you'll be promoted to senior designer. In two years, when they offer you a partnership in the company, you're going to turn them down flat, fly home to Colorado, start your own company, and knock everyone else down a spot on that best-of-the-best ranking list. But only after you marry me."

"That's exactly what I'm going to do," she choked out.

"Meanwhile I'm going to win that makeover contest, buy Maj back, start a large horse-training operation, and use Kajsa's soon-to-be-famous name to bring in the clients."

That earned him a laugh, though it sounded more like a shudder. "And I can design all your business cards and ads and anything else you need."

"You can take over as marketing director when you get back," he added.

"We'll have the most successful horse-training/graphic design business this side of the Mississsippi."

"The other side too."

She nodded, her eyes still glistening. "I'll be back."

"I know."

"I love you."

"I love you too."

She fished a small, black and white striped gift bag from her purse and thrust it into his hands. "I got you a goodbye present."

"I thought we agreed this wasn't a goodbye."

"It's more of a don't-forget-me-while-I'm-gone present."

Colton should have known she'd do something like this. He should have come prepared with a gift of his own. "I didn't get you anything."

"I didn't expect you to."

"But—"

She rose on her tiptoes and pressed a kiss to his lips. "I'll see you later, cowboy," came her whispered goodbye. Then she turned and walked away. Her pale yellow dress swished, her white sandals clacked, and her long blonde curls swayed.

Not once did she look back.

Colton watched the monitors until "On Time" became "Boarding" and then "Departed." Only then did he take the gift bag to the privacy of his truck and pull out the black tissue paper. He laughed when he saw Samantha's bright fuzzy green steering wheel cover nestled inside, along with a note that read: *I dare you.*

Without a second thought, Colton stretched it around his faded and cracked leather steering wheel and snapped it into place.

Twenty-three

UNDER THE EARLY, pale-blue Texas sky, The Will Rogers Memorial Center radiated an anxious, competitive energy as trainers checked in and settled their horses. Kajsa had to coax Maj into her stall and stroke her coat to calm her down while Colton stayed in the hallway right outside, sizing up some of their competition.

A smaller, chocolate mustang reared and whinnied while his older, plumper trainer lost his Stetson as he fought to rein in his horse. Down the way, a slender woman wearing a red, western-style shirt led her bay horse into the stall without any fuss at all. Her long blonde curls reminded him of Samantha and he quickly looked away, but not before the familiar pang of longing registered in his gut.

Colton had secretly hoped Samantha would hate her job, her boss, or her co-workers, but she'd taken to it instantly. Reading between the lines, she thought her boss walked on water and loved the hustle and bustle of New York. She'd even made friends with a few others in her complex already. The transition, it seemed, had been easy on her.

Colton, on the other hand, struggled. He missed her. Even though he'd stayed busy doing what he loved to do, he found himself counting down the days until he would see her again.

"Steady, girl," came Kajsa's voice from the stall. "I know you're excited to get out there and show those people what you can do, but it isn't time for that yet. You need to *calm down*."

Colton leaned against the stall door and folded his arms. A few weeks before the competition, Kajsa had informed him with a shaky, but very brave voice, that if Maj had to be sold, she wanted someone good to get her. Someone who owned enough land for Maj to run and could afford enough food for her to eat. Someone with lots of money.

"I want her to win," she'd said. "If she does, everyone will want to buy her and she'll be sold to the best person, right?"

"Right." Her eleven-year-old logic had charmed Colton. He, too, wanted Maj to win, but for an entirely different reason. The winning trainer would receive a check for five thousand dollars, which, if added to the three thousand they'd managed to earn so far, would hopefully be enough to buy the horse back.

His phone rang with Samantha's ringtone, and he quickly lifted it to his ear. "Howdy, city girl."

"Well? What's going on? Has it started yet?" Colton could hear voices and honking in the background.

"Not yet. They're still checking people in. It'll probably be another hour or two before anything happens. Where are you?"

"Oh, I offered to do the bagel run this morning so I could call and find out what's going on. I really hate that I can't be there." Her workload had been heavier than she thought it would, and she couldn't get away. That, and plane fare wasn't cheap. Colton hadn't been too surprised when she'd broken the news, but it still stank.

"I don't think you're going to miss too much," he said. "I have a feeling it'll be a lot of waiting around for only a few minutes of action."

"I still wish I could be there."

"Me too."

A horse whinnied down the way and bucked against the walls of his stall.

"Is that Maj?"

"No," said Colton. "Some horses still look like they're giving their trainers a run for their money and others look pretty behaved. It should be an interesting competition."

"How's Maj doing?"

"Let's ask the real trainer and find out." Colton raised the phone and his voice. "Hey, Kaj, how's she doin'?"

"Still over-confident and stubborn as always. Tell Sam I miss her."

Colton brought the phone back to his ear. "Hear that?"

"Tell Kajsa I miss her too. Where's everyone else?"

"Only Noah, Cassie, and Adi could make it. They're in the stands—or, at least they will be. Only the trainers are allowed back with the horses."

"I see." A moment of silence passed before she added, "I'm really sorry I can't be there. I miss you."

"I miss you too. Only seventy-seven more days to go," Colton said, referring to Thanksgiving weekend.

"Um, yeah . . ." She didn't do a good job of hiding the hesitation.

"What does 'um, yeah' mean?"

"It means I really hope so."

"You *hope* so? It's not a sure thing anymore?"

She let out a breath. "According to Stephen, the holidays are one of our busiest times. Most employees end up working the majority of the weekend, and those that do take off to visit family take a boatload of work home with them. So . . ."

Colton felt a sinking sensation in his gut. "So not until Christmas then."

"Probably not." She sounded as depressed as he felt, not to mention tired. "I'm so sorry."

Colton mentally added thirty days to his see-Samantha-again countdown, and the number shot back into the hundreds. Awesome.

Not.

"I need to pick up the bagels and get back to work," she said. "I'll call again during my lunch break."

"We'll probably be in the middle of competition by then, so I'll call you tonight after it's all over.

"Okay." She tried to sound perky, but Colton could hear the sorrow. "Tonight then. Good luck, cowboy."

"Thanks." The line went dead, and Colton shoved the phone in his pocket. Then he folded his arms, scuffed his boot against the soft dirt, and prepared for a long wait. During the next two days, one hundred trainers and horses would be scored on three components: the in-hand obstacle course, the riding course, and the overall condition of the horse. Between all of those events, they got to hang out right here.

Good times.

When Your Majesty's name was finally called, Kajsa squared her shoulders and led the horse into the arena. She walked over a bridge, through a darkened tunnel, and around some barrels, leading Maj through each obstacle. Then, with her hand on the mustang's shoulder, she coaxed Maj into lying down. She crawled into the saddle, gave the horse a pat on the shoulder, and Maj stood, taking Kajsa up with her. Thunderous applause echoed through the stadium, and Kajsa and Maj walked forward, stopped, took several steps backwards, and spun in circles. Twenty minutes after she led Maj into the arena, they rode out. Colton had never been more proud.

That night, under the bright, artificial lights of the

stadium, Your Majesty and Kajsa were selected as one of ten horse-and-rider teams to advance to the free-style finals on Saturday night. When Samantha heard the news, her squeal through the phone made Colton's ear ring for the next hour. The Mackies celebrated by taking Kajsa and Colton out for a barbeque-done-right dinner.

The following evening, during the free-style ride, Kajsa removed the saddle and rode bareback around the stadium, showing the judges how Maj obeyed her every command. Then she showed off her standing trick before dipping into an adorable cursty that Adi had instructed her she had to do.

"Boys bow. Girls curtsy," she informed her sister matter-of-factly.

Other trainers put on more of a show. One lassoed a cow while riding without a bridle, another led his horse across a small lake of inflated balloons, showing that the horse didn't scare easily, and another trainer jumped onto a moving flatbed trailer mid-ride. It was a pretty cool show that culminated with an awards ceremony.

Maj and Kajsa placed eighth.

Shoulders back, Kajsa remained stoic as she rode from the arena. But once Maj was safely secured in her stall, she crumpled.

"Hey now." Colton pulled her into a tight hug. "Out of one hundred professional trainers, you came in eighth, Kaj. That's amazing. Why the long face? You should be jumping up and down at how well you did out there. I can't even begin to tell you how proud I am of you."

She raised tear-filled eyes to his. "I wanted her to win. She's not going to go to the best home now."

"That's not true," said Colton. "Every single one of these horses will go to a good home, including Maj. You'll see."

The tears continued. "I'm trying to be brave, but I don't think I can watch someone take her away from me."

"I know. But I promise that everything is going to be okay." He pulled her close once more, hoping against hope that the three thousand would be enough to win back Maj. But the worst-case scenario had just happened. Maj had been a top-ten finisher, which meant she'd probably sell for a lot more than three grand, and eighth place wasn't enough to win them any award money. So Colton kept quiet and took Kajsa outside to the waiting arms of her family.

Early Sunday morning, they returned to the arena one last time, along with the ninety-nine other horses. The anxious, competitive energy from two days prior had dwindled into something that felt more like a funeral. Evidently Kajsa wasn't the only one who'd become attached to her mustang. No trainer looked very happy.

Horse after horse rode into the arena. The auctioneer gave a brief introduction, and the bidding began. Some of the lesser-trained horses went for four hundred dollars, others twenty-five hundred. The sixth-place finisher—a horse by the name of Butterick—sold for sixty-five hundred.

Colton's heart sank. At the rate the bids were going, there was no way they'd get Maj back.

Samantha chose that moment to call.

"Hey," he answered.

"Oh no. You sound depressed. Please don't tell me—"

"We're not up yet." Colton chose his words carefully, knowing Kajsa could hear everything he said.

"How much longer?"

"I don't know. Soon, I hope." The waiting was killing him. Come what may, he wanted to get Kajsa out of that stadium and back home to Colorado. She was tough, but not this tough. Bringing her with him had been a mistake.

"I'm staying on the line until it's over," said Samantha.

"I'm not sure my battery will last that long." Colton glanced around. There were still dozens of horses left to be auctioned. "Want me to call you back when our number is called?"

"Can I talk to Kajsa first?"

Colton handed the phone over. Kajsa nodded once,

twice, and the corner of her mouth actually quirked up before she said, "Love you too," and gave the phone back to Colton.

"I'm not sure what you said to her, but you sort of got a smile," said Colton, loud enough for Kajsa to hear. When she looked his way, he smiled and winked, but there was no quirking of her lips this time. Sometimes he worried she still blamed him for losing Maj.

Call our number already, he wanted to scream.

"Number sixty-eight, Your Majesty, ridden by Kajsa Mackie," the auctioneer finally said.

"We're up," Colton said into the phone.

Shoulders back and chin up, Kajsa coaxed Maj into the arena. The brief introduction came, and the bidding began. Kajsa didn't even glance into the stands. She stared straight ahead, reminding Colton of the day he'd driven Samantha to the airport. Maybe that's where Kajsa had learned it. But it was good she didn't look around. Otherwise she would have seen her father raising a paddle every so often, retaining the highest bid until it rose to four thousand. Then he shook his head and set the paddle on the seat next to him.

Colton clenched his jaw in frustration.

Next to him, a woman wearing a Mustang Makeover nametag waved her hand to get the auctioneer's attention.

"I have an anonymous caller on the phone," she said, pressing her phone to her ear. "He's bidding forty-five hundred."

"And we have forty-five-hundred," the auctioneer said in rapid-fire English. "Who'll give me forty-six?"

Someone in the stands raised a paddle, and the man on the phone bid higher. It happened again and again, until the anonymous caller won Maj for fifty-one hundred dollars.

"Sold to the anonymous caller," the auctioneer announced.

Kajsa turned the horse around to exit the arena, and a

single tear fell from the corner of her eye. Colton felt like crying right along with her.

"Well?" Samantha's voice came in his ear, reminding him that she was still there.

"We lost."

She didn't say anything. After all the effort, the hope, the waiting—it had all come to naught. Samantha didn't need to say anything. Her disappointment was felt all the way from New York.

"Kevin Grantham," the woman with the nametag was saying to the recorder. "G.R.A.N.T.H.A.M. He said he wants the horse released to the trainer, Colton McCoy. Yes, that's right. He would like to remain anonymous."

Colton stiffened for a moment then jogged to her side. "I'm sorry. What did you just say?"

The woman gave him a look that said, *It's none of your business.*

"I'm Colton McCoy."

"Oh." Behind wire-rimmed glasses, her eyes widened but she recovered quickly. "Well, it appears as though you will be taking Your Majesty home with you."

"We will?" came Kajsa's hopeful voice from behind.

The woman's expression softened. "Yes, my dear. The anonymous caller was bidding on your behalf. The horse is yours."

A smile that had been missing for way too long appeared on Kajsa's face. She leaned forward and wrapped her arms around Maj's neck. "Hear that, Your Majesty? You're coming home!" She looked at Colton, her expression radiant. "She's coming home!" Then she slid off Maj's back, handed the reins to Colton, and ran toward the stands. "I'll be right back. I have to tell everyone else!"

Colton glanced down at the reins in his hand and saw his phone. Oh shoot. Samantha.

He quickly lifted it to his ear. "Um . . . Samantha? You still there?"

"Oh, you're talking to me now?" she said dryly.

"You're never going to believe what just happened."

"I heard Kajsa, so I know it's something good. Did I hear Kevin's name too?"

"Yeah," Colton admitted. "Can you believe it? He wants to remain anonymous though, so keep it to yourself."

She laughed. "I'll keep it to myself, but it's only a matter of time before everyone else finds out."

"Why do you say that?"

"Kevin has a soft spot for the girls, and who else has the money to do that? I know my parents and Noah and Cassie don't," she said. "I mean, seriously. If Kevin wanted to stay anonymous, he should have bought Kajsa a bunny. Not a horse."

She made a good point—one that everyone else would probably deduce as well. "We'll have to find a way to give him all the money we raised."

"Anonymously, of course."

Colton laughed. "Kevin is a good man."

"Yeah, he is. He sort of reminds me of another good man I know."

Colton smiled. "Thanks, but I could never have bought Maj for Kajsa."

"Did I say it was you?" she teased.

"Who else?"

"Dusty."

"Dusty's not a man yet."

"And you are?"

"Of course."

"Great. Then you're man enough to come visit me."

Colton stiffened, not sure how to take that comment. Had she meant it as a joke, or had he detected a hint of a challenge in her voice?

A sigh sounded on the other end of the phone. "I'm sorry. I meant that as a joke, but it didn't sound that way. I just really miss you. This weekend has been tough, and I hate that I can't hop on a plane and come home."

"I understand," he said.

"Hey, listen. I've got to go. But give Kajsa and Adi a hug and a kiss from their sister, and tell Kajsa that I fully expect her to get that horse to let me ride her someday."

"Will do."

A slight pause and then, "I love you, cowboy."

It wasn't the first time Colton had heard those words, but this time it was different. Instead of the warmth and longing that usually accompanied them, it sounded more like a painful letting go. Colton didn't like it.

"Love you too," he said, because what else could he say? For the first time since Samantha had kissed him goodbye in the Denver airport, Colton wondered if the two year countdown would ever really come to an end.

Twenty-four

COLTON DROVE HIS shovel into the hard earth over and over again, tossing the loosened dirt to the side. It had been three days since his truck had ambled down the pot-marked dirt road leading to the McCoy ranch. Three days since his father had come out and greeted them with his hands on his hips.

"I had a feeling we wouldn't get rid of that horse so easily. How do you propose we keep feeding that animal?"

Kajsa gave his arm a pat on her way to get Maj out of the trailer. "Don't worry, Uncle Mike. I'll start teaching riding lessons to help pay for him."

That had been news to both Colton and his father. Good news. Kajsa's enthusiasm was back, and it was a beautiful thing.

Three days later, Colton went looking for his enthusiasm in the large, circular hole that his mother had asked him to excavate. She'd decided she wanted a fire pit, and Colton had volunteered to make it happen. Now that the competition was over, life had dulled, and driving a shovel into the ground gave him an outlet for his increasing frustration.

About lunchtime, his father showed up carrying a tall glass of ice water. He handed it to Colton who drank it down in several greedy swallows.

"How big did your mother say she wanted this?" asked his dad, surveying the hole, which, admittedly, had gotten a little out of control. Okay *a lot* out of control. It looked more like the makings of an in-ground hot tub rather than a small-scale fire pit.

"We need extra room for the gravel and retaining wall," Colton said.

His father raised an eyebrow. "You need two feet of gravel? How big are the bricks?"

"Oh, well . . . you know." Colton held his hands about two feet apart, exaggerating the measurements. "That big or so."

"No they're not. They're that big." His father pointed at a pile of smaller bricks by the corner of the house.

Colton shrugged. "Bigger is always better, right?"

"Not when it comes to forest fires."

Without saying anything more, Colton began shoveling dirt back into the hole. One shovel full, two, three . . .

"Somethin' on your mind, son?" his father asked, as though he had nowhere better to be than standing around, watching his son shovel dirt.

"Nope." Four, five, six.

"Keep that up, and you'll have to start excavating again soon."

With a sigh, Colton rammed the shovel into the ground and jumped into the hole to began compacting the dirt with the heel of his boot.

"You're actin' like you've got woman problems."

"Since when are women not problematic?" Colton muttered.

His father barked out a one-syllable laugh. "Isn't that the truth."

Pound, pound, kick, pound.

His father shoved his hands in the pockets of his jeans and swayed forward and back. "When it comes to women, I only have one piece of advice."

Colton wasn't sure he wanted to hear it. "What's that?"

"Simple. If it doesn't seem like she's worth the effort, she probably isn't."

The pounding stopped, and Colton squinted up at his father. What the heck was that supposed to mean? "And if she *is* worth the effort?"

His father made a sound that resembled a snort. "Then she is. And maybe you should do something about it." He ambled toward the house and swung open the screen door. It slammed shut behind him, leaving Colton with something entirely new to think about.

"Sam, you busy tonight?" a deep voice intruded on her thoughts.

"Why? What's up?" Sam frowned at the event postcard she was tweaking for a small engineering company in California. They were having a fall social and had contracted with Brecken Design to come up with the invitations, banners, custom napkin designs, labels for the food, etc. The job was low-profile, but it was the first project that had been given to her and her alone. Sam wanted it to be perfect. But there was something not quite right about the postcard. What? The font? The centered layout? The colors?

"Hello? Up here," said Derek, reminding her of his presence.

Sam pushed away from her computer and spun around to face him. No matter how late in the day it was, the man always looked perfect. Tall and clean shaven, with that sexy, laid-back vibe going on, Derek draped an arm over the top of her cubical. The slight wave of his dirty blond hair, the crispness of his fitted, button down shirts, the clear blue of his eyes—perfect. Too perfect. It made her wonder what he was hiding.

"Sorry. All yours now." Sam hoped he'd get to the point soon so she could finish the invitation and get out of here. Her parents would be arriving tomorrow night, and her apartment was in a chaotic state of . . . untidiness. The past week had been a lot of late nights and early mornings for work, and cleaning and laundry had dropped to the bottom of her to-do list.

"I was just thinking that we could grab a bite after work. Maybe take in a show?"

Was he asking her out? Had she done anything to hint that she *wanted* him to ask her out? Nothing came to mind. Then again, Derek was the sort of man who didn't need hints. One glance from him and most women went weak in the knees. But not her. She preferred Stetsons, Wranglers, and muscles that were earned the natural way—outside of a gym.

"Um . . ." Sam stopped herself from saying "I really wish I could, but . . ." because it was a lie, and instead said, "Sorry, I can't. My parents are coming tomorrow, and I've got a week's worth of cleaning to do if I don't want my mother to spend the entire weekend scrubbing my floors and washing dishes and telling me that I'm working too hard if I don't have time to tidy up a small apartment."

"Which is why you should come out with me tonight. Just a quick bite and then you might be able to twist my arm to help you clean."

Help her clean? *As if.* There was no way Sam would be letting Derek Lindstrom inside her apartment anytime soon. Maybe he really was as nice a guy on the inside as he looked on the outside, but Sam didn't trust perfect. Nor did she want to give him the wrong idea.

"Listen, I really appreciate the offer, but I'm going to have to say no. You should know I'm in a relationship right now."

"Yeah, I've heard the office gossip. I'm not asking you to be my girlfriend, only for the chance to get to know you better over dinner." He lifted his hands. "No hidden agenda here."

"Maybe another time." Oh, geez. Why had she said that? *Liar, liar, liar,* she told herself.

"That's your way of saying 'not gonna happen' isn't it?"

Oh good, he figured it out. Sam offered a sympathetic smile. "I'm already taken."

"I see." He didn't look overly happy at being rejected. "Well, when's this lucky guy coming to town? I'm sure we'd all like to meet him sometime."

He's not coming, Sam answered in her mind, trying to brush aside the stab of hurt that accompanied it. Every time she tried to remind herself that Colton had a very good reason for not boarding a plane to see her, a downer of a voice at the back of her mind would say, "If he really loved you, he'd come."

Was Colton thinking the same thing about her? Or did he understand the only reason she wasn't on a plane right now was because she had more work than she ever thought possible. That, and flights from New York to Denver cost about the same as the amount sitting in her bank account at the moment, and with rent due in three weeks there was no way she could afford a plane ticket.

"I'll take that as a 'you're not sure,'" Derek said. He withdrew his arm from the top of the cubical and pressed his lips together as though he had something else to say but wasn't sure he should say it. Then he cleared his throat and lowered his voice. "You're still young and single, Sam. And people change. Remember that."

Sam watched him walk away—the upright posture, the swagger, the confident way he'd looked back and gave her a nod, as though he'd known she'd still be watching.

She spun around and glared at her monitor, not happy with the seeds of doubt Derek had so easily planted in her mind. Colton wouldn't change. She wouldn't change. And this whole long distance thing wasn't going to change *them*. The reason calls between them had become a little more distant were because she and Colton were both busy, not because things were changing.

She frowned at her computer yet again, determined to get the invitation right—to do something that would make the not-right feeling in her gut go away.

Twenty-five

COLTON'S BOOTED FEET came to an abrupt stop before the gap of open air between the jet bridge and the airplane. His heart pounded, his breathing grew erratic, and every instinct in his body told him to turn around and go back to the safety of the terminal. His fingers tightened around his wallet that held a picture of Samantha, and he tried to remind himself why he was here.

Someone from behind lightly touched his arm. "Are you okay, dearie?" came a kindly, aged, female voice.

Colton looked over his shoulder to see a tiny, wrinkled couple behind him. He couldn't tell who was holding who up, only that the woman had reached out to him.

"I'm just . . . a little nervous about flying, that's all," he said. "Forty-five thousand feet above the ground is kind of high." Why Colton had googled average cruising altitudes for commercial planes, he had no idea. All it had done was sear the number into his brain like a silent alarm.

"Feel free to go ahead of me." Colton stepped aside, wondering where the couple had come from. He'd waited for everyone else to board ahead of him, and shouldn't they have been in the pre-board line?

As if reading his thoughts, the bald and age-spotted husband spoke up. "Pre-boarding is for the ancient, crippled, or young 'uns. Not us. It just takes us a bit longer to get down the ramp, is all. That's why we wait for the springier chickens to board first."

His wife leaned toward Colton and whispered, "I know we're old, but I don't want him to know that he's delusional, so I humor him." Her eyes crinkled even more when she smiled.

Colton liked them instantly. Someday he hoped that would be him and Samantha, only not at an airport about to step on a plane.

"We should go." The husband began to move past, but his wife resisted, holding him back.

"Is this the first time you've ever flown?" She peered up at Colton through thick-framed eye glasses, her short white hair framing her face in soft, thinning curls.

"Yes."

"Where's your seat assignment?"

Colton glanced at his ticket. "Um . . . 14C." An aisle seat. As far from the window as possible.

She continued to study him. "Why are you going to New York?"

Her candor charmed him, and Colton found himself answering. "To see my girlfriend."

"Is she worth it?"

Colton didn't hesitate. "Yes. Yes, she is."

Her smile widened, deepening the lines around her lips. She let go of her husband's arm and latched on to Colton's. "Well then. Let's get you to your gal, shall we? C'mon, Vern. We have a new mission." She dropped her voice again. "He likes missions. He thinks he's Tom Cruise."

"And she thinks she's as funny as Lucille Ball," came the man's ragged voice.

"I *am* Lucille," she quipped and she led Colton onto the plane. "Lucille Anne Monteray Dungworth. You only marry a man with that last name if it's true love."

Even though Colton's heart still raced and his forehead continued to perspire, he allowed the tiny woman to lead him on the plane and reconfigure a few seating arrangements so that he ended up in the middle of her and her husband. Without asking, Vern quietly lowered the window shade. They acted as though they often came across troubled, first-time fliers and knew exactly what to do.

Lucille took Colton's roughened hand in hers and gave it a pat. "I want to tell you a very interesting story about how I wooed Vern without him knowing it. Because back then, you see, us girls weren't supposed to do the wooing. I had to be sneaky about it, and I was. Vern didn't know what hit him until it was too late. Believe it or not, he really did used to look like Tom Cruise. Or I should say that Tom Cruise looked like him because Vern came first, though he won't admit it."

She continued to talk as the plane pulled away from the terminal. For the few, panic-attack inducing minutes of takeoff, her voice faded away, and Colton squeezed her hand as hard as he dared and tried not to think about the forty-five thousand feet of air that would soon be between him and the ground. But as the plane leveled out and the seatbelts-fastened light went off, his breathing evened a little, and Lucille's voice was there again, calming him down. Vern joined the conversation here and there, correcting his wife or adding something she'd forgotten, but mostly it was sweet little Lucille who got him to New York City.

As the plane coasted through the maze of LaGuardia and Colton's heart rate returned to normal, Lucille asked, "When do you fly back to Denver?"

"Tuesday morning. The 10AM flight."

She smiled and craned her neck to see her husband. "Hear that, Vern? He'll be on our return flight too."

Vern opened his mouth in what appeared to be the beginning of an argument then clamped it shut and grunted, looking resigned. Colton got the feeling they'd either be extending their stay or ending it early on account of him.

If it were anyone else, Colton would have tried to talk her out of it, but after listening to Lucille chat for a little over four hours, he knew that arguing with her wouldn't get him anywhere. If she wanted to be on his plane at ten o'clock Tuesday morning, she would be on the plane. And Vern would be with her because he loved his wife.

Outside the door of her apartment, Sam rifled through her too-large purse for the keys. But when all she could find was lip gloss, Tic Tacs, several receipts, a water bottle, and granola bar wrappers, she gave the bag a shake. A muffled jingle came from inside, and she went fishing again. "I know you're in there," she muttered. "I can hear you."

"You know that keys can't really hide, right?" said a voice that made Sam's knees feel like jelly and her heart skip several beats. Her fingers froze in her purse, and her feet slowly turned her around.

Four feet away, leaning casually against the wall in the narrow hallway, with his black Stetson, washed-out jeans, dark boots, and that almost-smile that made her insides turn to mush, stood the most handsome sight she'd seen since August twenty-fourth.

She squealed, dropped her purse, and plowed into him, wrapping her arms around his waist.

"You're here."

"I am."

"How?"

"How else?" He grinned. "Pony Express."

"Did the pony have wings and look like an airplane?"

He nodded. "I almost didn't make it but a really sweet, elderly couple talked me down from the ledge. They'll be on my flight home, too, if you can believe it."

"I can't believe any of it." Tears pooled in the corners of her eyes, and her head continued to shake as she digested what it all meant—what he meant to her. He was here. In Manhattan. *Here.*

His palms framed her face, and his thumbs wiped away her tears. "Two years is too long to wait, and New York is too far," he said.

"I know." It was too long and *way* too far, and holy moly, he was *here.* For how long? Why hadn't he told her? She would have left work earlier. She would have cleaned. She would have—

"I came for two reasons," he said. "To see you and meet with a manager at NYEC."

"NYEC?" Sam was having a hard time processing everything.

"New York Equestrian Center. They just opened an extension in Afton and need to fill some new positions. I happen to be a good fit for a few of them so they want to talk. We'll meet tomorrow, and if things go well, again on Monday. If they offer me a job, I'll spend the warmer months up in Afton and the winter months at their West Hempstead location."

Whoa, what? Colton was considering moving to New York? Since when? Why? How? *Overload, overload, overload,* screamed her senses. She took a step back and searched his eyes. "Afton?"

"A city about two hundred miles north of here. In pictures it looks a lot like Colorado. It's close enough we can see each other on weekends, and when I'm at West Hempstead we can see each other every day." He paused. "If you want."

"I . . ." Of course she wanted. She more than wanted. But he'd be giving up too much. It wasn't fair. "I can't let you do that."

"Why not?"

"Because . . . because I can't."

He took her by the shoulders and gave her a slight shake. "It's win-win, Samantha. NYEC is a pretty big operation, and I plan to come away with a lot of improvement ideas. It's a good opportunity."

"But—"

"But nothing. The ranch has been in our family for almost one hundred years, and it's not going anywhere. It'll still be waiting for us whenever we decide to go back."

We. It sounded so strong and permanent with no room for change at all, as though she and Colton were in this together no matter what. *Take that, Derek Lindstrom,* she couldn't help but think. *I told you I was taken. And so is Colton.*

"What about your family?" she said. "They need you."

"They'll be fine. I had a long chat with my parents before I made this decision, we all agreed that my brothers could use a lot more responsibility and Kajsa's itchin' to do more than muck out stalls and feed animals. Things will be fine back home. I promise."

"What about you? Will you be fine here?"

His dark eyes became pools of warmth and desire. "Do you really have to ask? I'll still be working with horses, and I'll be with you. Of course I'll be fine."

Her head felt like a bingo cage. Too many thoughts and feelings churned around and around and around. Guilt, excitement, worry, elation, what ifs, possible regrets—What was the right way to feel? Could she really let Colton do this for her?

"I don't know what to say," she finally said.

Colton's hands moved from her shoulders down her arms, causing an eruption of goose bumps to ripple across her skin. How she'd missed that feeling. How she'd missed him.

His fingers laced through hers. "Say you're excited," he said. "Say you still love me. Say you'll marry me."

Her breath caught. Her heart ceased beating. The hallway tilted on its side. "Marry you?"

His gaze remain fixed on hers. "I've had a taste of what life feels like without you in the everyday of it, and I don't like it. I want us to be together from now until we're old and wrinkly and delusional."

The pounding of her heart thudded in her ears. "I won't get delusional."

"I might."

"If you do, I'll pretend you aren't so you'll never know."

A smile lifted the corners his mouth, and he pulled her into a warm embrace. "Now I know we're going to make it. Say yes?"

Sam's heart swelled. The dingy hallway became bright and sparkly and dazzling. As if he had to ask. "Yes," she breathed.

"Good." His large hands cupped the sides of her face and his thumb traced the contours of her cheek as though he needed to remind himself what she felt like. And then he was kissing her, lightly at first, and then stronger, deeper, and harder, making up for all the weeks they'd spent apart. A powerful energy surged through Sam's body, brightening each dark crevice of her soul until not even a shadow existed.

Colton had flown to New York on an airplane, asked her to marry him, and was actually moving here. Sometimes miracles and magic and wishes really did come true.

A door opened and closed down the hall, and Colton pulled back slightly, still holding her face in his hands. "What do you say we take this reunion inside?"

"Yes, let's."

Sam nodded a hello to the Latin American guy who lived a few doors down then dug through her purse once again, this time finding her keys.

Colton followed her inside and hung his hat on the hat

rack before looking around. "Looks nice. Where's the rest of it?"

She grinned, gesturing to the room. "You're looking at it. There's the kitchen, the not-so-great great room slash bedroom, and through that door is the tiniest bathroom you'll ever see. Welcome to Manhattan."

Colton's arms came around her waist from behind, and his chin rested on top of her head. "Compared to this, The Shack is a mansion."

Sam laughed, and it echoed through the space, sounding almost foreign, like her walls weren't sure what to do with the noise. She felt like she should warn them. *If Colton's coming, be prepared to hear that sound a whole lot more.*

She turned around and wrapped her arms around his waist, hugging him close. Life couldn't possibly get any better than this.

Her father once told her that she would only be as happy as she made up her mind to be. Over the years, Sam had taken that advice seriously, always trying to seek out the good, the fun, the friendly; to find something to smile about even when the world looked gray and dreary. Most of the time, she was successful at it, always thinking her life was pretty darn full. But that was before. Before summer. Before the ranch. Before her attempted fling with a cowboy.

Now, happiness had a new benchmark, and its name was Colton McCoy.

Other books in the Meet Your Match Series . . .

Prejudice Meets Pride (Book1)

After years of pinching pennies and struggling to get through art school, Emma Makie's hard work finally pays off with the offer of a dream job. But when tragedy strikes, she has no choice but to make a cross-country move to Colorado Springs to take temporary custody of her two nieces. She has no money, no job prospects, and no idea how to be a mother to two little girls, but she isn't about to let that stop her. Nor is she about to accept the help of Kevin Grantham, her handsome neighbor, who seems to think she's incapable of doing anything on her own.

Prejudice Meets Pride is the story of a guy who thinks he has it all figured out and a girl who isn't afraid to show him that he doesn't. It's about learning what it means to trust, figuring out how to give and to take, and realizing that not everyone gets to pick the person they fall in love with. Sometimes, love picks them.

Rough Around the Edges Meets Refined (Book 2)

For Noah Mackie, life is finally back on track. He has a great support system, a promised promotion is on its way, and he's finally getting the hang of this single father thing. But when the job falls through and his neighbor's match-making efforts become more aggressive, Noah is in for yet another unwanted detour. With his career and two spirited daughters to worry about, he doesn't have time for dating—especially not someone like Cassie Ellis, his girls' beautiful and sophisticated dance instructor, who is about as open and approachable as a brick wall.

Rough Around the Edges Meets Refined is about two people who think they know exactly what they want but who have no idea what they really need. It's about learning that people aren't always what they seem and that sometimes life's detours take you exactly where you need to go.

If you're a fan of period romances, you may also enjoy my regency series . . .

If you'd like to be notified when future books are available, feel free to sign up for my New Release Newsletter at RachaelReneeAnderson.com.

Dear Reader,

Thanks so much for reading! I hope this story took you out of reality for awhile and into a world of escape and rejuvenation because everyone deserves that once in awhile.

If you're willing, I'd love a review from you on Goodreads or Amazon or wherever else you'd care to post one.

You can find me online at RachaelReneeAnderson.com.

Thanks again, and happy reading!

Rachael

Acknowledgements

A massive thanks goes to Karey White, Kathy Habel, Sheralyn Pratt, Braden Bell, Rebecca Talley, and Karen Porter. I love and appreciate you all for your honesty, encouragement, friendship, and help. This book would be in a sorry state without you.

And, as always, a special thanks goes to my family—particularly my husband, Jeff, for your love and support. You make me feel very blessed.

About Rachael Anderson

A *USA Today* bestselling author, Rachael Anderson is the author of six novels and three novellas. She's the mother of four and is pretty good at breaking up fights, or at least sending guilty parties to their rooms. She can't sing, doesn't dance, and despises tragedies. But she recently figured out how yeast works and can now make homemade bread, which she is really good at eating. You can read more about her and her books online at RachaelReneeAnderson.com.